THE EROTIC POTENTIAL OF MY WIFE

David Foenkinos

The Erotic Potential
of My Wife

Translated from French by
Yasmine Gaspard

TELEGRAM

London San Francisco Beirut

First published in France by Editions Gallimard in 2004 as
Le potential érotique de ma femme
This English translation published in 2008 by Telegram

ISBN: 978-1-84659-045-0

This book is supported by the French Ministry of Foreign Affairs as part of the Burgess programme run by the Cultural Department of the French Embassy in London. (www.frenchbooknews.com)

Liberté • Égalité • Fraternité
RÉPUBLIQUE FRANÇAISE

A full CIP record for this book is available from the British Library.
A full CIP record for this book is available from the Library of Congress.

Manufactured in Lebanon

TELEGRAM

26 Westbourne Grove, London W2 5RH
825 Page Street, Suite 203, Berkeley, California 94710
Tabet Building, Mneimneh Street, Hamra, Beirut
www.telegrambooks.com

For Victor

How to reach you, sensual wave,
You who give me wings ...

M

In vain, reason denounces to me
the dictatorship of sensuality.

Louis Aragon

A Kind of Life

I

Hector had the face of a hero. One felt he was always ready
to act, to face the dangers of our vast humanity, to ignite
the feminine masses, to organise family holidays, to hold
conversations in lifts with his neighbours, and, if truly
feeling in good shape, to understand a film by David Lynch.
He was a kind of hero of our times, with chubby calves. But
there he goes deciding to commit suicide! What a hero
he's turned out to be. An acquired taste for the dramatic
had made him opt for the Metro. Everyone would know
of his death, it would be like the media preview of a film
that's bound to flop. Hector listened politely to the tannoy
announcements telling him not to buy tickets from touts;
something useful to remember should his suicide attempt
fail. Not knowing anything about him yet, we hoped a little
for this failure, even just to know if it was possible to judge
someone by appearances alone. It's crazy what a hero's face
he had. His vision was blurring, thanks to the sedatives
he'd swallowed. Better to die sleepy. Ultimately this proved

lucky. Hector passed out, eyes vacant. He was discovered motionless in the corridors of the Metro, closer to Châtelet-Les Halles than to death.

His slumped body resembled an aborted foetus. Two paramedics who looked like doped-up athletes (we are wary of faces now!) came to deliver him from the eyes of commuters delighted to witness a plight worse than their own. Hector was thinking of one thing only: in failing in his suicide, he had condemned himself to live.

He was transferred to a hospital that had been freshly repainted. Sensibly, 'fresh paint' could be read everywhere. He was going to have to spend several months here, bored to death. Very quickly, his only pleasure became a cliché: staring at the nurse while dreaming vaguely of stroking her breasts. He was drifting to sleep thinking of this, while at the same time admitting to himself that she was ugly. In this vegetative state disgrace seemed mythical. This judgement seemed too harsh; the nurse did appear sensual between two shots of morphine. And there was this doctor who passed by from time to time, like people pass by in a party. These encounters rarely exceeded a minute. It was necessary for the doctor to take care of his reputation by looking busy (it was about the only thing that he *was* taking care of). This incredibly tanned man would ask him to stick out his tongue in order to come to the conclusion that he had a beautiful tongue. It was good to have a beautiful tongue, it felt good to have a beautiful tongue, but a fat lot of good that would do Hector. He was not quite sure what to expect, he was a great depressive who was whimpering from the bottom of a pit. It was suggested that family or friends be contacted if 'sir' had any. (Discreetly, the possibility of hiring some was put forward.) These options were rejected by less-than-polite silence, but let's skip over that.

Hector did not want to see anyone. More precisely, and like all invalids, he did not want anyone to see him as he was now. He was ashamed to be a fraction of a man between nothingness and less than nothingness. He occasionally called a friend, making believe that he was abroad: 'The Grand Canyon is just wonderful, what ravines!' Then he would hang up, because he was the Grand Canyon.

The nurse found him pleasant; she even told him that he was an *unusual* man. Would you want to sleep with a woman who found you unusual? Now that is a key question. Ultimately, no. Let's just say that women never sleep with him. She was interested in his story; well, what she knew of his story, that is, his medical file. It is not saying much that there exist more glorious selling points. Does she exist, the woman who will offer you her body because she likes the way you never miss your DT Polio booster? 'Oh, how you turn me on, precise man of vaccines!'

Often, the nurse would rub her chin. In those moments, she took over the role of the doctor; to be sure, there was room for this role. She would then come much closer to Hector's bed. She really did have an erotic way of repeatedly caressing the white sheet with her hand, her well-groomed fingers like legs on a staircase, climbing its whiteness.

Hector was released at the beginning of March, though essentially the month had no importance, actually nothing had any importance. The concierge, a woman whose age could no longer be deduced, feigned to have been worried by the tenant's absence. You know, this way of being falsely worried, this way of imagining yourself back in 1942, with a voice so high-pitched that, close to a railway track, it could derail a train.

'Mister Balanch*iiiine*, I'm so happy to see you! You see, I was so worr*iiiied* ...'

Hector wasn't naïve; he had been absent longer than six months, so she was trying to score her Christmas presents. He feared taking the lift in case he bumped into a neighbour and had to explain his absence. He dragged himself up the stairs instead. But his heavy breathing alerted his neighbours, who pressed their eyes to the peepholes in their doors. As he made his way, doors opened. It was not even Sunday. This building was tiresomely idle. And there was always an alcoholic neighbour – with whom he shares as many points in common as two parallel lines – who forced him to drop in on him. Just to ask 'How's everything going?' three times, and for Hector to respond 'Good, and you, how's it going?' each time. Unbearable familiarity. After convalescence, it would be nice to live in Switzerland. Or better even, to be a woman in a harem. He faked liver pains to excuse himself, but inevitably his neighour would ask, 'Tell me you didn't bring back cirrhosis from your travels, did you?!'

Hector managed a smile and continued his journey. He opened the door, turned on the light. Nothing had moved, obviously. But Hector could feel that many lives had passed, he could smell the reincarnation. Dust had watched over the place, before boredom drove it to reproduce. You could inhale the procreation.

Night fell, like every evening. He made himself a coffee to give his insomnia an air of normality. Sitting in his kitchen, he listened to cats creep along the gutters; he didn't know what to do. He was thinking about all the mail he hadn't received. He glanced over at a mirror he'd bought in a second-hand shop; he could distinctly remember that day, and the memory scared him. Just as the scent of a person can be smelt by looking at a photograph, the fever he'd suffered that day overpowered him once again. The important thing was not to think about it; he was cured. Never again would he go to a second-hand shop and buy a mirror. He looked momentarily at his reflection. His face, after six months of convalescence, seemed different. For the first time in his life he imagined his future to be stable; of course, he was mistaken. But nobody here wanted (yet) to contradict him. But before moving on to his future, we need to linger on his less-than-perfect past.

2

Hector had just unexpectedly experienced the greatest moment of his life; he had come face to face with a 'NIXON IS THE BEST' badge from the 1960 US Republican primaries. It was a well-known fact that post-Watergate, Nixon badges were rare.

His connoisseur's nose twitched delicately, like the eyelids of a teenage girl whose breasts grow faster than expected. This discovery would enable him to win the national competition for the 'best holder of electoral campaign badges'. It is something few know, but collectors gather for competitions. (It is a real pleasure to share this knowledge.)

At these events, collectors fight about rare stamps and coins in an atmosphere that is as festive as it is dusty. Hector had registered in the badges category, a surprisingly popular category that year (due to the upsurge of pin amateurs, purists stuck by the badge). One had to have nerve to reach the quarter-finals. Hector didn't show any sign of nerves, he knew he was superior, and, in a cosy corner of his memory, he relived the moment of the Nixon discovery. He was walking, hands in front like antennae, with a fever in his step. The collector is a sick person permanently seeking a cure. For two days he drifted, desperately seeking a badge; it had already been six months since he had obsessed on badges, six months of wild passion, six months where his life had been nothing but badges.

One should always beware of Swedes who are not blond. Hector was impassive. At any moment he could whip out the 'NIXON IS THE BEST' badge in front of the Swede's luminous eyes, eyes that were reminiscent of the suicide rate in Sweden. Even if his name was impossible to remember, his sublime performance the previous year was impossible to forget, because Mister was the reigning champion of electoral campaign badges. In his civilian life, the Swede was a pharmacist in Sweden. It was said that he had inherited this profession – a collector's professional life often fits like an oversized suit. As for their sex life, it is as calm as a dunce during school holidays. Collecting is one of the rare activities that doesn't rely on seduction. Accumulated objects are barriers like a horse's blinkers. Only flies can see the cold sadness that emanates from their eyes, the sadness that is forgotten during the euphoria of a competition.

The Swede, at that moment, was even forgetting the very word 'medicine'. His parents – who raised him with the love that a syringe has for a vein – suddenly held no sway. The public held its breath, it was one of the most nail-biting finals ever to grace us. Hector met the look of the Pole he had eliminated in the semi-final. He could sense his anxiety, that he still had not accepted his defeat. Hector wondered how the Pole ever thought he stood a chance with a Lech Wałęsa badge.

The Swede's empty head held few distractions, so he remained calm. He rubbed his temples from time to time; it was so obvious how he was trying to destabilise our Hector. Ridiculous attempts. Our Hector was strong. After years of collections, he was sure of his Nixon; it would certainly have warmed Nixon's heart to know that Hector would win thanks to him. Nevertheless this wouldn't make it into the history books and it wasn't likely that the night's performance would diminish the blight of Watergate. However, things proved not so simple. (Remember: do not trust Swedes who are not blond.) The bastard brought out a Beatles badge. The public stifled their laughter. But far from being fazed, the Swede explained that it was a campaign badge for head of the 'Sergeant Pepper Lonely Hearts Club Band'. The poor man must have got word of Hector's Nixonian jewel and had not found another tactic than to confuse the jury – Swedish vermin. And his plan seemed to be working, since the jury (in all honesty, a bearded man) began to smile.

Hector protested, but in a way that can only be described as ridiculous: he clenched his teeth. He didn't know how else to protest. But let's cut to the chase: the cheat's tactic was found very original, and Hector was declared the loser. He handled it with dignity, making a slight head movement towards the winner and then leaving the hall.

Alone, he began to cry. Not because of his defeat, he had

already had so many highs and lows, and he knew that a career was filled with such moments. No, he cried because of the absurdity of the situation; to lose to the Beatles was laughable. It made him realise his entire life was absurd. For the first time, he felt the strength to change, a strength that would allow him to break free from the crazy cycle of collecting. His whole life, he had been but a heart beating to the rhythm of his discoveries. He had collected stamps, diplomas, paintings of moored ships, Metro tickets, first pages of novels, plastic drink mixers and cocktail sticks, corks, moments with you, Croatian maxims, Kinder Surprise toys, paper napkins, charms, rolls of film, souvenirs, sleeve buttons, thermometers, rabbits' feet, birth certificates, seashells from the Indian Ocean, noises at five in the morning, cheese labels; in short, he had collected everything, and every time with the same excitement. His existence was frenetic, with spectacular periods of pure euphoria and extreme depression. He could not recall any moment of his life where he had not collected something, where he had not been looking for something. Nonetheless, with each new collection, Hector always thought it would be his last. But systematically, he discovered in his fulfilment a source of non-fulfilment. He was the Don Juan of things.

Parenthesis

This last comparison is the right one. People often say that there are 'ladies' men'; Hector can be thought of as an 'objects' man'. Not to compare women to objects, but obvious similarities can be noted, and our hero's anxieties can be reflected in the anxieties of two-timers, and of all men transfixed by feminine rarity.

Ultimately, it is the story of a man who loved women. Hector was sometimes torn between two collections. Some examples: after six months of a life dedicated to cheese labels, he would suddenly fall for a rare stamp, and be devoured by the impulse to leave everything for this new passion. Sometimes the choice was physically impossible, and Hector endured months of anguish juggling two lives. It was then necessary to keep each collection at opposite ends of the apartment, and massage the feelings of individual items. Hector conferred human attributes to these objects. He often witnessed the jealousy of a stamp towards a birth certificate. Admittedly, these were times when his mental health left most to be desired.

In addition, each collection stirred different emotions in him. Some, such as the pages of a book, were more sensual. Some collections, sensitive ones, of great purity, once gone, became fabulous sources of nostalgia. And other more carnal collections, one-night collections, so to speak, touched on more brutal and physical spheres. That's what it was like with the cocktail sticks. One cannot make a life with a cocktail stick.

Of course, he had sought treatment before to prevent himself from starting a collection, to abstain; but nothing helped, it was stronger than him. He would fall for something and feel the irrepressible need to collect it. He had read books; all told of the possibility of repressing or exorcising a fear of abandonment. Some children who are neglected by their parents choose to collect as a form of reassurance. Abandonment is a time of war; the fear of lacking leads to accumulation. In Hector's case, it could not be said that his parents had neglected him. Nor could it be said that they had smothered him. No, their attitude stagnated between the two, in a kind of timeless lethargy. Let's see.

3

Hector had always been a good son (we have seen, and, in some cases, appreciated how he approached his suicide attempt with discretion; there was something caring in telling everyone he was in the United States). He was a good son anxious to make his parents happy, to lull them into the illusion of his success. In front of their door, he put the finishing touches on his smile. His eyes were ringed by rings. When his mother opened the door, she did not see her son as he was but as she had always seen him. If our family relationships are films seen from the distorting closeness of the first row, Hector's parents were seeing them from inside the screen. A parallel can be drawn between the need to collect and the need to be noticed as a *changing being* (one could simply say *living*).

We will return to this hypothesis later.

By and large, we will return to all hypotheses later.

The composure required not to shatter the myth of the accomplished son is formidable work. These things are easier to imagine than to achieve. To make believe that we are happy is almost more difficult than to actually *be* happy. The more he smiled, the more his parents relaxed; they were proud to have such a happy and caring son. They felt as good as when electrical household appliances outlive the end date of their guarantee. In the eyes of his parents, Hector was a German brand.

Today, he finds it more difficult than ever. Admitting to the suicide attempt is on the tip of his semi-blue lips. For once, he would like not to pretend, to be a son in front of his parents, to cry tears large enough to wash away the pain in a torrent. There's nothing he can do; as always the smile on his face blocks and fetters the truth. His parents were always passionate about their son's interests. For them the word *passion* is a flash feeling, an orgasm of the smile. ('Oh really? You found a new soap holder ... That's fabulous!') And it would stop there. It was real enthusiasm (Hector had never questioned it), but it seemed to perch perilously on the peak of a Russian mountain, and after exposure, it fell dramatically into a silent void. No, that is not quite right: his father occasionally tapped him on the shoulder to express his pride. Hector, in these moments, wanted to kill him; without really knowing why.

Hector ate at his parents' even when he was not hungry (he was a good son). Meals took place in silence hardly disturbed by the gentle slurping of soup. Hector's mother liked making soup so much. Sometimes, our lives should simply be reduced to one or two details.

Here, in this dining room, no one could avoid the grandfather clock. Noise of terrifying loudness, and precision, owing to the precision of time, could make you go crazy. It was this movement that punctuated the visits. This loud movement of time. And the waterproof tablecloth. But before the waterproof tablecloth, let's focus on the grandfather clock.

Why do pensioners love noisy clocks so much? Is it a way of savouring the remaining crumbs, of relishing the last slow moments of a beating heart? Everything could be timed at Hector's parents'; even the time remaining for them to live. And the waterproof tablecloth! The passion of all these old people for waterproof tablecloths is just incredible. Breadcrumbs feel at peace there. Hector smiled slightly to show his appreciation for the meal. His smile resembled the dissection of a frog. Everything was stretched out, grotesquely, to accentuate the traits as though they were coming directly from a pop-art painting. This likeable absence of finesse is a common trait of belated children. His mother was forty-two at his birth, and his father almost fifty.

Somewhere, a generation was skipped.

Hector had a big brother, a very *big* brother: twenty years older than him. It could be said that his parents' obsession was the polar opposite of accumulation. They had contemplated Hector's conception (which gave a subject to this tale, so thanks are due to them), the day that Ernest (the brother in question) left the nest. One child at a time. And if menopause had not taken away this theoretical momentum, Hector would have had a younger brother or sister who would surely have been called Dominique. This concept of the family was taken as original, and as often with everything that appears original, nothing is. We were in a place that was barely exciting, a place where time is required to understand things. This surpasses all praise for sluggishness. To summarise: Ernest was born, he had made his parents very happy, and when he was leaving they had thought: 'Hold on, that was good ... And what if we made another?' It was as simple as that. Hector's parents could never concentrate on two things at once. Ernest was very shocked when told the news, he who had dreamed of having a younger brother or sister when he was a kid. Having a child as soon as he left could have been considered sadistic, but, as we know, sadism wasn't their style.

Hector saw his brother once a week when he came to eat the family soup. It felt good to be a foursome. There was the atmosphere of a Bach quartet, minus the music. Unfortunately, these meals did not linger. Ernest talked about his business, and no one ever knew the right questions to prolong his stay. They had a certain incompetence in the art of rhetoric and conversation. Hector's mother – let's call her by her name this time – Mireille (writing this, we realise we always knew she was called Mireille; everything we had learned about her was typical of a Mireille) dropped a tear when her older son left. Hector was jealous of this tear for a long time. He understood that no one cried for him because he returned too soon. For a tear, the separation needs to be at least two days. It would've been almost possible to catch Mireille's tear, weigh it, and know exactly when Ernest would

24

come back; oh, this is an eight-day tear! A heavy tear, the bubble of depressive lives, through which we see Hector in the present time, this time of narrative uncertainty, to face a terrible epiphany: though he is now an adult and comes to slurp soup once a week, his mother does not cry for him. Suddenly, her weightless tears are the heaviest burden that his heart has ever had to bear. We are faced with the certainty that his mother prefers his brother. In a strange way, Hector almost feels good; we must try to understand, it is the first time in his life that he finds himself faced with a certainty.

Our hero knows that what he feels is wrong; it is palpably simplistic. His parents have a stunningly narrow range of emotions. They love everyone the same. It is a simple love that extends from a sponge to their son. This good son, thinking himself the least favourite, had treacherous thoughts towards his parents, hatred even. Some days, he dreamt that his father gave him a couple of hard slaps; the image of a red mark on his skin would have made him feel alive. At one time, he had thought of provoking reactions in his parents by becoming a problem child; he never dared to in the end. His parents loved him; admittedly in their way, but they loved him. Therefore he had to play the role of good son no matter what.

Parenthesis about Hector's father in order to know why his life is only moustaches, and outline a theory that considers our society exhibitionist

His father sighed from time to time, and these sighs revealed the extent of his role in his son's education. In the end, it was better than nothing. This father (let's say it straight: this Bernard) had sported a moustache very early on. It was in no way indicative of a carefree attitude, as many people would lead us to believe; a lot of thought had gone into this moustache, it was almost an act of propaganda. To understand this Bernard, let's allow ourselves a short break, it will last as long as a sigh. Bernard's father, born in 1908, died heroically in 1940. The word 'heroic' is a great mantel. Everything can be hung on it. The Germans had not attacked yet, the Maginot Line was still virginal, and Bernard's father and his regiment had a small village in the east under siege. A small village where there lived a woman weighing 152 kilos who wanted to profit from the regiment's passing. Though men usually didn't want her, she had more chances in times of war, in times of abstinence. To cut a long story short, Bernard's father decided to attack the mountain, and due to the sliding of a sheet, in a rotary motion whose horror we do not dare to imagine, there occurred what is commonly referred to as suffocation. This story (quiet now!) had been spared from his family, by masking everything with the word heroic. His son was only ten. Bernard was thus raised with the cult of his father as a hero, and slept underneath a portrait that covered that of the Virgin Mary. Every evening and every morning, he blessed this face curtailed by death, this face adorned by a moustache full of vitality. We do not know exactly at what moment the damage took place that led Bernard to be marked by his father's moustache for the rest of his life. He prayed to no longer be smooth-cheeked, and sanctified his first hairs. When his face had the honour of accommodating a dignified moustache, he felt himself become a man, become his father, become heroic. He had relaxed with age, and wasn't angry upon noticing a certain virgin terrain on his sons' upper lips; each lived the life of hair he chose. Bernard thought that all men had become beardless, and that it was a mark of our modern society. He liked to repeat that *we live in the least moustache epoch there is.* 'Our society cuts the hair, it is pure exhibitionism!' he shouted. And always, after these rants, he would return to his intimate thoughts, encumbered by nothing.

During his uneventful adolescence, Hector regularly visited his brother. He sought advice from him to better understand their parents. Ernest told him that there was no user guide, apart from 'maybe making Mum believe you love her soup'. He should not hesitate to resort to the little respected domain of the sycophant when he wanted to go to a sleepover. ('I think I will need to take a thermos of your soup, Mummy.') Except that Hector had no friends, at least not friends that would invite him to sleep over.

His relationships were limited to trading cards in the playground. No sooner had he reached eight years old that his reputation as a formidable collector was established. Thus, Hector asked for advice from his brother, and very quickly this brother became his mentor. It is not that he wanted to be like him, but he was like him. More precisely, he looked at his life telling himself that it would perhaps belong to him. Everything relied on this 'perhaps', because in truth his future was a blur to him, it was a paparazzi's shot.

Ernest was a big dull man who had married a short rather exciting redhead. Hector was thirteen when he met his brother's future wife, and he dreamed that she would take charge of his sexual education. He didn't realise that our lives had become twentieth-century novels; the epoch of the epic deflowerings of the nineteenth century had ended. He masturbated wildly, thinking of Justine, until the wedding day. Family – there was something sacred in that idea. A short time later, Justine gave birth to little Lucie. When her parents were working, he often babysat the little girl, and played dolls with her. He could not believe that he was someone's uncle. And faced with that child, he was unable to conduct a perfectly normal life; in the face of innocence, we see the life that we are not living.

Hector had studied law without being very dedicated. Nothing interested him apart from making collections. (If only collecting could be a career!) He was hired as an assistant in his brother's firm, but since he had not graduated, this post risked being the pinnacle of his career. In a way, this was a relief, as he then would avoid the anxieties of career planning and, even more of a relief, the office politics of all these lawyers with teeth that needed filing. He had noticed that success always comes with beauty; certain female lawyers had breasts and legs that would ensure them magnificent appeals. Hector would shrink in his chair when they passed next to him; of course this was useless, because even if he'd been two metres tall they still wouldn't have noticed him.

In any case, women only interested him in the obscurity of his bedroom a few minutes a day. He sometimes cheated on his masturbation by going to see a prostitute, but this did not have much importance for him. During all these years, women were resting in the back-room of his excitement.[1] He would look at them, admire them, but did not desire them. Well, let's be frank, when Hector believed he did not desire women, he actually believed that he could not arouse desire in them. He would repeat that his time was completely taken by his passion for collecting; even if anyone doubted the evident evidence, we could still bet the first lover of his body would sweep him into a horizontal position.

He thanked his brother for getting him a job, and this brother mechanically answered: 'Between brothers, you have to help each other.' Hector was lucky to have a big brother that was like a dad.

Let's go back to when Hector was eating his soup. He has not been to visit his parents for six months. They are not looking at him. The atmosphere is incredibly jovial, his return is a day of celebration. What joy to see him again after such a prolonged trip! 'And Americans, do they sport moustaches?' worried Bernard. Like a good son, Hector detailed the incredible moustaches of Californians, blond and bushy like Scandinavian kelp. They were swimming in good humour, a beautiful good humour where cheerful croutons could be dipped, and it is within this feeling of latent happiness that Hector had the idea that it might be

---

1   We make an exception here for the six days of a semi-torrid fling with a Greco-Spanish woman.

time to tell the truth. It was less an idea than being unable to contain his suffering any longer. His heavy heart could no longer bear it. For the first time he would be himself and not hide behind the ill-fitting costume his parents had designed for him. He would be relieved, and would finally be able to end the masquerade and not suffocate anymore. When he got to his feet, his parents looked up.

'So, I have something to tell you ... I tried to commit suicide ... and I wasn't in the United States, but in convalescence ...'

After a moment of silence, his parents started to laugh; a laughter that was the opposite of eroticism. 'That was so funny!' They clucked at their chance of having such a gentle and comical son – Hector of Hectors – comical son! This son who had (what's the word?) a slight credibility problem. He had been classed in the 'good son' category, given that he came to eat even when he was not hungry. And good sons do not commit suicide; in the worst case, they cheat on their wives when she goes on holiday to Hossegor. Hector stared at his parents, there was nothing nuanced to read in their faces; their faces like telephone directories. He was condemned to be their cliché. In their eyes he saw the reflection of who he had been the day before. This bond imprisoned him indefinitely.

His mother loved to accompany him to the doorstep, like a stewardess at the end of a flight. He almost felt the urge to say thank you, while promising to fly again soon with this airline. The soup airline. Once downstairs, he always needed to walk a few metres to no longer hear the heralding tick-tock of death.

4

Hector is in the trough of the wave, in the trough of the ocean, in the trough of the Universe. There is good reason to feel small.

After this blasted semi-final where it was concluded never to trust Swedes who are not blond, he had cried about the absurdity of his life. However, a positive feeling emerged from his disgust: and it is from disgust that one can progress. Hector found a bench; once seated his ideas began to stabilise. The pathetic floated all around him. Hector could see apparitions of Swedish heads, so much so that he had to close his eyes to avoid a Stockholmian whirl-wind. Nixon was nothing but a good-for-nothing who had really deserved his Watergate. Nixon was his moment of hitting rock-bottom. Hector sighed and made a major reso-lution: he would stop collecting. He had to try to live like everyone else, hold off and not accumulate things anymore. In the flash of a moment, he felt as relieved as never before, and yet it only lasted the flash of a moment, because the memory of all the previous resolutions that he had never adhered to came to his mind, like a depraved undertow. All those times he had promised himself, on his knees crying, to stop everything. And every time he had fallen off the bandwagon, seeing a coin, then another, then another. His conclusion was simple: in order to abstain, he had to stop accumulating altogether, to stop having twos of anything, to concentrate zealously on uniqueness.

We were at the beginning of 2000, which was a handicap for Hector. He could not stand Olympic years, judging them nefarious for all the meagre exploits the rest of us try to achieve. He especially resented that collectors' competitions weren't recognised as Olympic sports. (Even if only to be humiliated by a non-blonde Swede – as long as it took place under the Sydney sun.) He was trying to occupy his thoughts, so as not to have to confront his struggle at that moment. He went home, and put his calendar on his desk. He noted the date: 12 June, day one of the Olympics. He clenched his fist as though making a passing shot on a match-ball.

Afterwards, he spent a more or less peaceful night.

And even dreamed that a brunette whispered to him: 'Make a wish and that's it.'

On the difficulty of concentrating on uniqueness

The next morning, he made his first mistake by turning on the television. Almost all products were offered in twos. There were even 'two-for-one' offers and his heart began throbbing. He changed channels and landed on TV-Shopping where the moderator was explaining that for 'one more franc' we could have a printer with the computer; might as well say that one franc was nothing but symbolic dust. Nowadays, to sell a product, two needed to be offered. We had gone from a consumption society to a double consumption society. And, as for glasses, they were flogging four pairs in so-called box sets for all seasons, as though the sun had become an all-powerful celebrity in front of whom you need to accessorise accordingly. In this particular case of quadruple consumption, the active incitement to collect was flagrant, criminal.

Later that morning, Hector went to work. With a certain dose of anxiety, he confessed his resolution to his brother. Ernest kissed him hard and hugged him as hard; he was proud of him. If their parents have never really grasped the seriousness of the situation, on the contrary, Ernest had always been very worried by his little brother's passion: no sex life, a professional life that solely relied on familial support ('Between brothers, you have to help each other'), and hours spent accumulating cheese labels. In spite of his big size, Ernest was quite sentimental. He dropped a tear. In the throes of his emotion, he assured him of his full support, and of all his love. 'You have to admit your illness before beginning to heal.' He loved saying these momentous slogans. Then he went to deal with a case of the highest importance. He was one of those in charge at Gilbert Associate and Co. (pronounced Guilberrte – it's English), a firm founded in 1967 by Charles Gilbert. Those in charge of Gilbert Associate and Co. often had to deal with cases of the highest importance.

At work, everyone liked Hector. He was an exemplary employee who always did his work with a smile. If young women did not look at him, women who were not as young were moved by (it should be confessed) his pretty lamb's head. When the news of his resolution did the rounds of the firm, a great unspoken compassion surrounded the brave Hector. Employees had witnessed the collector's frenzied crises on many occasions; he had often left traces of his fever in his wake. And this unspoken compassion turned into a telethonesque compassion. The whole afternoon people came to pat him on the back, and many offered him their tuppence worth. 'Good luck,' 'Our hearts are with you,' 'My brother-in-law quit smoking last week,' 'My wife no longer satisfies me in bed'; in short, he had the privilege to listen to all the weaning experiences of the legal milieu. He was the spoiled child of the day.

A secretary who was almost as much a redhead as she was old placed a basket on Hector's desk; it was money! There had been a collection to encourage him in his ordeal. In the US collections are customary for operations not covered by Social Security (because there is no Social Security) and, as a result, dollars were often gathered for kidney transplants and such like. In a way, Hector was having a life transplant. That evening, in his room, Hector stared at the money and reflected that this sum was the price to pay for healing. It was a thought that did not mean anything, but he was seeking to fill himself with musings verging on incoherence to avoid thinking about any stamp or cocktail stick. As he had the habit of counting sheep before falling asleep, he was rather unsettled. To fix things, the sheep was followed by a horse, then the horse by a seahorse, then the seahorse by a red squirrel, then as our goal is not to make our reader fall asleep, we end here this enumeration which lasted a good part of the night. For the record, it was the otter that knocked him out.

The days passed without a hint of collecting. Hector began to believe in his until now unused aptitude for quitting. Nevertheless, people warned him: 'The first days are always the easiest.' (His brother's sentence, of course.) Days were made easier because he suddenly found himself at the heart of a wonderful enthusiasm. People sought to support him like a political candidate, the lawyers were careful not to ask him anything twice the same day. And a secretary was assigned to ensure that he never dealt with files that were too similar to each other. Hector took on the role of royal child who systematically had to be entertained in different ways. We could wonder why there was such collective enthusiasm. It is true that they all had affection for him, but was that a sufficient reason?

It seemed that it was not. In a super-competitive professional context stuck on appearances, an employee's weakness (more precisely, an employee who poses no danger to the hierarchy) unites rivalries in one fell swoop. Hector was like a new coffee machine in a tyre factory. A new social fabric was materialising around him. And, to top it all, what was happening was not escaping the eyes of the director of human resources, who would soon preach what he considered a radical method: nothing was worth more for the profitability of a company than hiring a depressive in an underling position.

The love around him and the meddling of others in his struggle had the perverse effect of destabilising him. Like a true French sportsman, he began to fail under the pressure; this pressure that consisted in not deceiving. He cried in the men's room, and put toilet paper under his eyes as not to make any noise. He who had been so strong and merciless during so many negotiations, he who had mastered the art of Chinese bluff and neuropsychic concentration, was literally breaking down. He felt weak, without armour. To change his life, it suddenly seemed to him, he would at least have to die.

Hector left the office early. In the street, his legs were hesitating like first-time lovers. On impulse, he ran into a post office. He came out of it, relieved for a few seconds, with a series of insignificant stamps. Philately, my God, was the worse of the collections! If he was going to come off the bandwagon, why not do it with something more original! 'Stamps, stamps,' he could not stop repeating the words that were hurting him so much. Why not coins as well? It was an easy, pathetic relapse. He retraced his steps, wanting to change his destiny, with the illusion that he merely had to retrace his steps to erase his recent acts. Back in his office, with the nauseous aftertaste of the stamps still in his mouth, he was unable to get back to work. Thankfully, something happened. Géraldine (the redhead secretary) walked towards him swaying her hips in her usual way that certainly figured in the best days of the 'Winter 54' collection. Hector watched her in slow motion; her woman's mouth opened.

5

'Hello, my name is Marcel Schubert.'

'Like the composer?' asked Hector, trying to be convivial, and saying the first thing that came to his mind. 'No, it's spelt Choubert.' Once the preliminaries were done with, something happened in the expressions of these two men, something gentle and intimate, something seeming like the evidence of a friendship.

Choubert was Géraldine's nephew through marriage. She had come to see him because she knew that this nephew had suffered from compulsive hoarding in the past, and that he had come out of it. She had merely suggested that they meet, and Choubert had appeared in front of Hector saying: 'Hello, I am Marcel Schubert.' He had a clear advantage over Hector, as he had not changed collections since 1986. He had a stable passion and presently lived in a quasi-humdrum frenzy. He worked in some bank or another that, thanks to honest bonuses, allowed him to appease his passion. His parents had gone to live in Venezuela (his father had become ambassador as he had not managed to finish writing a novel before the age of thirty) and had left him a sumptuous 65-square-metre pad in the Second Arrondissement in Paris. After a short walk one could reach the Stock Exchange. At the time when the Berlin Wall was crumbling, he had met a Laurence, and they had been building a relationship ever since. Some must know Laurence since she was an attacking player in the ping-pong team whose performance was appreciated during the world championship in Tokyo; the others will get to know her later. The couple had not wanted any children, it was a choice like any other. They sometimes received guests for dinner in an atmosphere that was always very pleasant. When the mood was excellent, jokes could be expected from Choubert as the dishes were being washed in the kitchen.

This was a happy life.

The principal information that Marcel divulged to Hector was that there existed meetings of Collectors Anonymous. They took place every Thursday on the first floor of a discreet building. The concierge thought they were a sect, but, greased with gifts, she had stopped thinking about it at all. Hector listened to Marcel; for the first time, he was with somebody who could understand him. From the following Thursday, he went with him. Hector introduced himself to the eight people present at the meeting, and all expressed sincere compassion. He explained how his life had been an absurd chain of absurd collections. His confession relieved him, but far less than listening to the others. The aim of the *Collectors Anonymous* meetings was in fact not to feel isolated anymore. Healing became possible as soon as the suffering of others was acknowledged. It was also the strangeness of all these meetings: what seemed like the height of mutual assistance was the most egotistical enterprise there is.

Thus strange discussions could be apprehended:

'I had a great "howlophilist" period until March 1977, just before I became a "keyboardophile".'

'Oh really, you were a "keyboardophile"?'

'Yes, I needed to reassure myself, to hang on to something.'

'That was certainly better than being a "skylightophile"!'

'Oh, how funny!'

This is just a sample of the pre-meeting ambience. Then everyone would sit down (except the one who was collecting moments of when he was standing), and Marcel led the debates. Everyone spoke in turn, and more time was spent on those who had relapsed during the week. It was adorable. With regard to Hector, everyone agreed that he would come out of it quickly. He was young and the illness had been detected in time. For others (and here we think especially of Jean, completely addicted to miniature trains and to lighters) there was not anything more that could be done – they were euthanising themselves gently during the meetings. And there were also these two Poles who had the strangeness of collecting appearances of two Poles in novels. Their case seemed especially desperate.

That night, Hector did some push-ups, surprising his muscles. He slept on his left side, life was going to be simple. The following days, he did pretty well at work, he received encouraging remarks from his superiors, and women's legs made his heart beat faster. He went to see the secretary without whom he never would have met Marcel, and offered her 142 porcelain spoons, vestiges of his collection. She was very moved, and her emotions spread easily. And it was already the day of the second meeting: Hector, upright, and with a certain pride, announced almost not having thought about collections at all, and he was applauded. There was delight in others' delight, a real solidarity reigned. After the meeting, Marcel suggested a day trip on Saturday to see the sea. And also to inhale it, said Hector. Yes, to inhale it. In all honesty, Marcel was a bachelor this weekend as Laurence had a ping-pong congress – well, a kind of reunion of ancient 'pongist' combatants at a chateau in Sologne.

Saturday, Marcel was poetic in front of the sea. Contemplation of the horizon was giving his voice wings. You see, Hector, that whale far away, that is your illness ... and together, by uniting our spirits, we do everything to attract this whale to the shore ... when your illness berths it will be a beached whale. It was so beautiful out that they ate mussels. Marcel ordered champagne even though Hector did not really like champagne. Hector did not want to displease him. Marcel was the kind of person who speaks loudly, and who slaps his friends' backs. Not having an athlete's physique, Hector clenched his bum cheeks during these moments of beautiful friendship. During dessert, Marcel asked his new friend how he envisaged his life after collecting. Hector could not imagine anything, and especially not the future. Marcel insisted, and suggested a beautiful life with a dog and a wife. You know, Laurence has pretty friends, you must like athletic women, their backs are a bit too hard, but they're pretty. If you want, we can introduce you to one. Hector did not want to have wicked thoughts, but it sometimes occurred to him, in the flash of a moment, that Marcel's life must be seriously boring for him to invest himself so much in his. These were wicked thoughts of course; Marcel was a pure soul.

Marcel collected hair. Women's hair, obviously. A lucky man, he rejoiced in having a corner dedicated to his passion in his apartment, and Hector had the privilege of visiting this sacred spot. He overdid his enthusiasm slightly so as not to vex his friend, going as far as adding a few 'ahs' and 'ohs', well executed for a novice of deceit. He resented the pressure on those who are told confidences. It must be noted that a collector is recognisable by the notable lack of interest he holds in others' collections. In an insidiously friendly way, Marcel was also seeking to test the convalescent Hector. The first piece in the collection, 'redhead vintage' 77' immediately provoked respect. Hector thought that hair without a woman was like a hand without an arm; following the magic of women's hair leads to a crash in an atrocious void. Hair does not have the right to be an impasse. Marcel launched into an explanation of the '70s. Let's listen. He estimated that no other period had been as 'hair' as the mid-70s. No one could offer a counterpoint; those years had incontestably been *very* hair'. The *worst* period for the bald. Hector, during the development of the Marcellian theory, remembered his father and his fascination for the moustache.

Blondes from 1983 and 1984, eternal brunettes from 1988, and the auburns from a few days ago were all perused. Hector, to be courteous, asked him how he had procured all these wonders for himself. Marcel admitted that he had an arrangement with a hairdresser from a neighbouring street. 'He calls me as soon as he spots a rare specimen, and I go there to filch the treasure.' Unique and easy collection, no anxiety, there were only benefits. On that note, Laurence came in and offered to make dinner. Hector yawned but it was not enough for him to escape. He allowed himself the indiscretion of asking his friend whether his wife was jealous of his collection. Laurence jealous? This was so nonsensical that Marcel could not even muster a laugh. Laurence was not jealous, and Laurence was preparing a roast that she had kept for her return; it was one of her peculiarities, she loved eating a roast after returning from ping-pong. 'Perfect,' said Hector. In any case, he didn't have a choice in the matter. They were offering him a mandatory Martini in the guise of an aperitif. Marcel looked him straight in the eye and announced with solemnity: 'I have presented my collection and my wife to you ... You really are a part of my life!' Hector was moved to *really* be a part of someone's life, but he could not help feeling uncomfortable. He had not yet dared to admit that he was not crazy about roasts.

Laurence called Hector. She wanted to get to know his culinary preferences, more precisely his preference for cooking time, so he went into the kitchen. Oh me, well you know ... He did not have any particular taste. She came towards him as though she suddenly wanted to stare at him, Hector could no longer make out the details of her face, especially not the active tongue that she had just stuffed in his mouth. Simultaneous to this oral aggression, she fondled his testicles. Then, pulling back just as suddenly, she said loudly: 'Very well, I'll make sure it's rare!'

Hector mumbled and blamed it on the Martini. Nevertheless, he felt the irrepressible urge to help himself to another drink. Drinking avidly, he closed his eyes so as not to see the face of the friend he had just betrayed, this friend who was showing him his collection and presenting him his wife. Hector was vermin. Wives were being presented to him, and he offered his testicles. It took him some time to realise that he had been sexually assaulted. A word was stuck in his mouth, an obvious word, but nonetheless a word that did not dare come out: nymphomaniac. My God, Marcel lived with a nymphomaniac. This same Marcel approached him, and as though he could read his guilt, he asked: 'Do you think my wife's attractive?'

He hurriedly answered no, before realising the tactlessness of such a response. He lamentably retracted his answer to a yes, of course. Hector was no social ace. Why was this happening to him? He was sweating. Marcel approached his ear to whisper that women who play ping-pong had a magical way of fondling, 'erm, well you know what I mean.' Hector was reanimated with some slaps, and Marcel accompanied him home.

Marcel tucked him in, and insisted that Hector call him

at any time in case of emergency. He had quite a bad night, he was tormented by images of old collections, he dreamed of overflowing wardrobes where he did not lack anything. He clung to these dreams, and could not stand opening his eyes again. But someone was ringing his doorbell early in the morning; and the bell was far too insistent to pretend not to be there. An enormous box was delivered that, once left in the living room by the sweaty courier, lorded it like a dictator after a putsch. He opened it mechanically to fall face to face with two thousand corks, give or take, from champagne bottles. And at the top, a card on which was written:

Monsieur Honoré Delphine, deceased on 12 October, has left you his collection of corks.

This time, he could not pull himself back together. There he was, trying to be a man like any other, but still people were sending him corks. There were always dead people who were sufficiently bored to try to ruin lives; feeling so lonely, they tried to hasten the demise of the living. Destabilised by a fondling of testicles, finished by a collection delivered by a courier, he had to end this life that was heading towards a mirror, modelling itself on his past. How could he know at that moment that he should hang on to find out its strange outcome? His movements were becoming blurred, and he rushed to the Metro, to play out the scene of his failed suicide attempt and, additionally, the beginning of our book.

Six months later, our pseudo-hero was coming home from the United States, that large country he knew as much about as happiness. The concierge tried to score her Christmas presents, and an alcoholic neighbour (a pleonasm if ever there was one) tried to hold him back. Once seated at home, we had stopped to go back in time. Hector did not sleep a wink that entire night. After six months of convalescence, he needed to find the courage to return to a normal life. This was the turn of phrase that the tanned doctor had used: 'Normal life, old boy, you are returning to normal life.' It was necessary to at least try to commit suicide to be called 'old boy' by a doctor. Normal life, life without collections. This time, he was cured. He could not really say how, or at what precise moment, but during all his time in the clinic, he had washed himself of his past. He felt as though the particles of another man had parachuted inside him.

His brother called him to ask what he intended to do. He had allowed him to obtain a long sabbatical, but now that he had done a comeback, he needed to tell him when he was going to go back to work. He did not dare tell him that the real reason for this pressure was that he was missed! Without him, the firm had taken on a ruthless appearance, like an episode of *Dallas*. Hector requested a further week's holiday for a peculiar reason: he did not at all have the look of someone who has just returned from the United States. And to look like your journey was important nowadays. In any case those who have been there say *States*, and the longer their stay, the more they stretch the '*a*' to mark a certain intimacy that the rest of us are unable to understand: '*Staaaaaaaaaates*'. This intimacy is interpreted as proof. He therefore needed a week to learn everything about the United States. One week to go back to work, cured, and with a concrete alibi for the not very glorious six months of convalescence.

At the François-Mittérand Library he asked for the United States section, and ended up in the Geography department. Hector enjoyed letting his finger slide on the spines of the books as he remembered an old collection, without any palpitations. How could he have been so stupid? He hesitated to do some push-ups, just to generate some instant pride. Finally, he came face to face with the *Atlas of the United States*. He stretched his arm, and this same arm collided with another arm. You needed to follow this other arm to see that it belonged to a human sample of feminine origin. He had just entered a competition with this woman for the same book. Polite, she was the first one to apologise. Gentlemanly, he insisted that she take the book. The union of politeness and gentlemanliness had the following conclusion: they would share the book, they would sit together and they would try not to step over each other when turning the pages. On the way to the sofa, and without really knowing why, Hector thought back to a Croatian maxim that said that we often meet the woman of our life in front of books.

Manifestly, there was a book there.

'So you're interested in the United States?' she asked.

'Yes, I've just come back from there.'

'Oh really, you were in the *Staaaaaaaaaates*?'

'Yes, and I have the feeling that you were too.'

They were swimming in the points in common and the coincidences. And to back up this good fortune, each one contributed his comments, while glancing over at the *Atlas*. Yes, Boston, it's magnificent, it's a good agglomeration of 8,322,765 inhabitants. And Kansas, it's crazy the way how it's crossed by the Bluewich Meridian. In short, globetrotting mythomania was being flaunted. And it would only have taken one of them to have really gone to the United States to realise the other's con. When two people lie to each other about the same subject, there are few chances that they will be unmasked. It was then that Hector committed the fatal error of asking his atlas partner why she was so interested in the United States. She explained to him that she was a sociologist. It is a word that muddled him so much that it took him a while to understand that she had just retuned his question. They were almost playing ping-pong. He was lost. He did not know what to say; and as often happens when we do not know what to say, we say the truth.

'I want to make people believe that I've been there.'

He thought that she would take him for a madman, but what she thought to be mad was this coincidence. She also wanted to make people believe she'd gone! Fired up, Hector asked the name of the young lady and, amazingly, he was confronted with a Brigitte. And in a totally weird way, he had needed to know her name to find her beautiful. He never admired the unknown, and the name of a woman reassured him.

Before panicking him completely.

Brigitte, that was promising; a little weird, but why not? We unfortunately never have the choice of the names of the people we meet. It was the kind of woman who makes you want to drink tea. That first night, she would think of Hector again. They had promised to see each other the following day. Brigitte was not in the habit of meeting people in the street, even less in libraries, even less with the same intentions regarding a book. She would probably sleep quite badly, with more awakenings than events in her life. We did not really know much about Brigitte. Surely she had not been unhappy, her parents were adorable pensioners, her brothers and sisters adorable brothers and sisters. And above all she had sumptuous calves.

All the same we need to know one thing. Like an enchantment, a mystery surrounded Brigitte. As a child, she had fallen asleep on grass, grass long since dead. She had let her mind wander, and her little girl's eyes had harnessed the wind, and the future, and some reminiscences. Her thoughts that day had been as gentle as successive awakenings and slumber. A butterfly had then judged it wise to rest on her nose, and in close-up Brigitte had contemplated the majesty of its movements. It remained on her nose a long time, large and docile. Brigitte had seen the world behind the butterfly; its wings, almost translucent, had formed a magical prism. When it took flight again, Brigitte's eyes followed it the longest time possible. She was perturbed for a long time by the moment when she saw the world through the filter of a butterfly. She was afraid everything would seem ugly to her afterwards. But nevertheless, she had drawn a strange conviction from this magic moment. It was the certainty that she was gifted with a rare power; that a unique ability had just developed inside her and would reveal itself one day.

They were so sweet during their date the next day. It was up to the man to speak, and the man was Hector. As she had referred to sociology, he asked her: but why *sociology*? She wanted to smile, but not feeling entirely comfortable (it would surely take twenty-six days for her to relax), she explained that she was studying '*solitude in an urban environment*' in the framework of her doctorate. Hector repeated '*solitude in an urban environment*', overstressing an air of intrigue. Yes, it involves spending six months in Paris with no social relations. So, she had told family and her few friends that she had spent six months in the United

States. They would not have the temptation of disturbing her on the other side of the Ocean.

'I have not spoken for six months. That's also why my mouth was a bit dry yesterday,' she clarified.

'Oh I see,' said Hector.

After this vivacious answer, they decided to work together. Fake travellers to the '*Staaaaaaaaaates*' had to help each other. They sat in big armchairs to revise. Their knowledge of the United States was relative to their desire to see each other. After a few days, they were under the obligation of creating new states.

For the first time, Hector worried about whether he was attractive. He looked at himself at length in the mirror, and bought himself a tie. He decided to speak to Marcel about it, as he was a specialist in women, at least in the capillary part. Marcel had never been as happy to be somebody's friend. At the bar where they met, there was even an order for alcoholic beverages. The place was reminiscent of a giant Turkish bath. Marcel was shouting a bit too loudly, gesticulating all over the place, and it was his way of implicating himself in Hector's love life. He really took this mission to heart, and beneath his airs of an alcoholic adventurer, beneath his airs of a Russian athlete, beneath all his airs, a sentimental air could be unearthed. The very fact of evoking the potential entry of a woman in his friend's life made tears rush to his eyes. Although he was meant to be reassuring and advising, it was Hector who had to raise his spirits; sentimental stories always filled Marcel's heart, they sprinkled it with rose petals.

At the library's exit, Hector and Brigitte formed a couple. Without really knowing what fate wanted from them, they positioned themselves side by side, facing life. It was one of these moments preceding love where people unveil themselves in the innocence of the obvious. Hector spoke about his past as a compulsive hoarder, Brigitte confessed having had spots until the age of seventeen and a half, in a nutshell they were laughing foolishly, like all those who we have seen laugh foolishly in parks; it is one of the rare moments where idiocy is a positive attribute. A new life was now revealing itself, and to celebrate it in a burst of poetry, there was at that moment the charm of a ray of light after an angry dark sky. Hector gained self-assurance just by looking at Brigitte. He felt important, like a limousine leaving an airport. Brigitte, usually ensconced in her restraint, allowed herself to be transported, without yet really knowing the erotic potential that was wastefully dozing in her.

Erotic potential, the expression was enticing. Indeed, we were entering the immediate hope of sensuality. Brigitte, never nominated elsewhere, was standing at the front of the stage. The last time Hector had seen a naked woman was on a television screen. The idea of sex was like a fish that wakes up with legs. The future lovers had spoken little since their exit from the library. Brigitte's apartment was located on the top floor of a building in the centre of town, the noise coming from the street cradled the room, the co-owners had recently voted for the installation of a lift. They were allowing themselves to slide into love. Hector acted like he was used to this type of thing by partially drawing the curtains; of course, he dreamed of being in the most complete darkness. He was afraid that their bodies would not be at the height of their encounter. He stayed in front of this window, an instant, an instant that was becoming rather long, an instant that was not really an instant anymore but the outline of eternity. Behind him was the body of a woman that was no longer hidden by anything. Hector had heard the sound of feminine clothes vanishing into the ground, this sound of nothing that justifies men having ears. Hector lifted the sheet; Brigitte was naked. In front of the beauty of that moment, he collapsed while remaining standing; his spinal column slid towards his feet. In the face of this emotion, Hector was flesh with no foundations. He laid his body on her body, and placed his lips on her lips. Everything was then but an affair of silence. A silence like the beginning of processions; each felt as though they were making love with a church.

Some minutes later, Hector was enveloped by the uneasiness of sudden happiness. Brigitte also did not feel comfortable; she clenched her fists. After long methodical breaths, they made love again. Many, many times again. At nightfall, Hector got dressed; he wanted to walk under the stars. Brigitte kissed him on the landing. As soon as he was outside he thought again about the shoulders of this woman he wanted to love madly, the nape of her neck in the afternoon. He then began to stagger; feelings gnawed at his legs. He allowed himself several detours before going home to stretch his legs, dizzy in his happiness. He was thinking about Brigitte's body again, he wanted to see her under a magnifying glass, raise her skirt in the lift and slip himself between her thighs. The body of the other, the body of the woman, what is the word? He felt as though he had suddenly become pure. We progress through the body of the other; it is through the body of the other that we become innocent.

Hector's night of wandering ended in the office. His brother arrived on the dot at the time he arrived every day. He was surprised to see him so early. He was sick of waiting, he had walked all night! He wanted to see his brother to announce the big news. His wedding, yes, he was going to get married to Brigitte! Ernest paced up and down, it was the least distance required to express his frenzy. He brought out his address book to notify everyone; hello, are you sitting down? After two hours, cursing himself for not knowing more people, he began a new round of his address book, and announced the wonderful news yet again. At Gilbert Associate and Co., a reception was organised to celebrate the event. There was a spread of appetisers, and Hector did not flinch in front of the cocktail sticks. Of course, Marcel was invited. (Laurence could not free herself because she had a vital training session before a vital competition.) Champagne arrived triumphantly at six, and people kissed him a lot. There were many great 'hip, hip, hip, hoorays' for Hector. Finally, he was asked the name of the lucky lady. And it is at the precise moment when he pronounced the name 'Brigitte' that he remembered not having notified the lucky lady of his intentions.

A strange paradox had been torturing Brigitte the whole day: it was during her total immersion in urban solitude that she had met the man, seemingly, of her life. She hesitated to change the subject of her sociology thesis, and then considering happiness to be a selfish matter, she had preferred to protect her fundamental discovery: to find love you have to seek solitude.

Hector's brain, completely stuck in Brigittian flavour, had neglected that one of the particularities of marriage is to unite two people. That did not really matter anyway, wasn't this irrevocable proof? You could always forget to announce your intentions when they were flagrant. It was a fact, they were going to be married. And that evening when they met for their second night together, the matter was simply outlined. Shall we get married? Yes, let's get married. What simplicity, this Hector and this Brigitte! They were like Swiss heroes. Sexual pleasure developed all aspects of its incipient hegemony. Brigitte's calves were themselves surprised at their Olympic suppleness, Hector discovered himself an adorer of ear-lobe nibbling. Underneath the sheets, they became anonymous. They practised saying *yes* in all languages. The next day at lunchtime, Brigitte would be peeling leeks, and the peels would be fascinating.

Lovers always feel two emotions skimming gentle hysteria. First, they discover all the good qualities in life. Suddenly, the daily routine goes on a diet, and the worries that were the encumbering existence of every respectable single person disappear in a new lightness. Life seems beautiful to them with the same lack of lucidity they will feel later when they go into rapture about the beauty of their ugly baby. The second feeling is a great intoxication. Hector for instance savoured the expression 'my wife'. He used it whenever he could. He only had to be asked the time in the street for him to answer 'I don't have it, but if my wife was here ... my wife has a beautiful watch ...' Brigitte took on the mystique of Mrs Columbo to Hector's Detective Columbo. Placing 'my wife' in every sentence was disconcertingly easy. He could also innovate by veering into the international. An American *hors-piste* skier incontestably remained the climax of the pleasurable, nothing was chicer than a 'my wife' nicely thrown in. Soon, Hector would surely dare the mythical 'you fuck my wife'; happy as he was, it would not take him long to take himself at least for Robert De Niro.

But before anything else, he had to meet Brigitte's brother. He had always played the role of decision-maker in the family. He was a kind of Godfather, minus the hand-kissing. Even Brigitte's father did not take any decision without previously discussing it with his son. Gérard did not have many neurones, but he did have very beautiful thighs. He had participated in the acclaimed Paris-Roubaix race, but had unfortunately fallen on a rock that had hammered in his skull. Added to the doping from previous years, this fall had ended by turning him into a vegetable, so much so that certain gossipmongers called him 'the Turnip'. There was something unfair in this label, and the ungrateful had quickly forgotten Gérard's hour of glory when he had climbed onto the podium of Ouarzazate-Casablanca. It was always very easy to criticise after the deed. Brigitte's family had remained focused on this victory. It was a shame that no image of the exploit had been taken. Only a magnificently framed photo on the parents' sideboard attested to the performance. This photo where Gérard was surrounded by young men, slightly paltry but forcedly combative, and brandished a trophy in the wind and dust (the gossipmongers who called him 'the Turnip' claimed that this photo had been taken at a studio in Bobigny. What slander!). It was this heroic image that made Gérard the incontestable leader of the family. In other words, to have a chance of officially possessing the woman of his life, Hector had to bone up on his cycling history.

Luck was decidedly not leaving him, as he had the privilege to have the son of Robert Chapatte as one of his acquaintances, albeit very far removed. In a few meetings, he had transformed himself into an unbeatable expert on the gear ratio, and still could not understand how Laurent Fignon had allowed the Tour '89 escape him to the benefit of Greg Lemond because of a few cursed seconds. Brigitte was proud of her sporty future husband. She was not worried about what turn the summit meeting between the two men of her life might take. Hector was dressed to the nines (he was so lacking in confidence that he even had doubts about that number); and his yellow tie was turning pale. All that was left was to find his welcome posture. It is well known by all competitors that everything is in the first look; you have to know to take the ascension even before the first whistle. While Brigitte was preparing stuffed tomatoes in the kitchen – her brother's favourite dish – Hector sat on the couch, stood up again, settled by the window, tried to smoke, but that did not look sporty so he placed a hand on the table to look nonchalant, acted surprised, frankly wanted to absent himself. Sweating, he was seeking the ideal posture, when suddenly, without really knowing how it found itself there, an idea crossed his mind. A brilliant idea, that of the *hands behind the back*.

The door rang.

Gérard came in and discovered the one who was postulating for the honorific role of brother-in-law. Surprise was immediately perceptible in his eyes. Hector had had a stroke of genius. It was so strange to be greeted by a man with his hands behind his back. He almost looked like a butler; the notion of deference was on offer. This attitude was incredibly touching, his bust leaning forward like a lead soldier, he did not know how to react to the hands behind the back. But our Gérard was not the kind to encumber himself with anything other than the fleeting echo of a surprise. He walked towards Hector, with a heavy step, the step of a man who had formerly climbed the steps to the podium of the Ouarzazate-Casablanca race. Once again, and like in all the big moments of his life, there was the ambiance of desert and dry throat; this meeting felt mythical. Brigitte and the stuffed tomatoes remained silent. Hector, hands behind his back, was doing everything not to look petrified; he attempted a smile that was finally only the jolt of a zygomatic bone at the end of its life.

It was then that the following occurred.

Hector was not used to putting his hands behind his back. He had never been stopped by policemen and he had never made love with the Mistress of the Dungeon. So inevitably, his *hands behind the back* profited from their new view and froze to glean time from the outrageous hegemony of the *hands in front of the legs*. In other words, and for almost two seconds, an eternity for this situation, Gérard's right hand remained suspended in solitude. Brigitte was worried: but why does he not extend his hand? How could she know that Hector was a victim of vengeance from the *hands behind the back*? Vengeance that he managed to suppress with a big mental effort, and finally his right hand unblocked itself. Only, it shot up so fast from behind his back (a crazy pace) that it did not manage to stop at the height of Gérard's hand, and aimed straight for his nose, where it crashed violently.

Gérard stumbled backwards, a little like how the Tower of Pisa will in 152 years, 14 days and 12 minutes.

For the briefest moment, Brigitte thought this gesture was intentional. How could Hector explain the involuntariness of his act? The clumsiness of a hand that pushes a vase can be excused, but how can a hand that lunges towards a face be excused? Should he admit to the crass anarchy of his hand's movements? Gérard got back to his feet abruptly but was far too shocked to react; deep down, he respected Hector's act. Not having understood that it was an atrocious accident, he deemed this man to have balls, and that he deserved to marry his sister immediately. Hector sweated out his last drops of sweat. Gérard touched his face. His nose was not broken. Only a bit of blood hesitated, but it was noble blood; Gérard always coagulated courteously.

Hector did not oppose Gérard's version of events during dinner. He remained convinced of the gesture's intentionality (an analysis that would bring him a good number of problems in the coming months, as he would systematically punch every new person he met). Brigitte discreetly explained to Hector that her brother was like that, he often analysed things in a peculiar, even off the mark, way. Gérard went home, and profited from the full moon to wander along the riverbanks. The fist he had taken slap-bang in his face was making him romantic. He was recollecting the scene, and trembled with emotion and pride at the idea that his sister would marry a big shot like Hector. The movement of that hand had propelled the evening to the ultra-select sphere of unforgettable things. This beautiful encounter had just entered his personal history to sit against the indelible memory of the Ouarzazate-Casablanca podium.

That night, Hector tried the missionary position.

7

Via Gérard, Brigitte's parents were taken body and soul to Hector's cause. On the other side, with Hector's parents, things would only be pure formality, as long as Brigitte liked the maternal soup. Hector dreamed to see in his parents' eyes what he called *sentimental consideration*. He wanted to be perceived as a future devoted husband and father, the kind of man capable of organising decent summer holidays, taking everyone's leisure activities into account. Hector was fidgety, it was the first time he was bringing a girl home. He was hoping for a sparkle in his parents' eyes, a derailment in the routine of their dreary affection from this great novelty. If he longed for his father to see him as a man, he especially wanted for his father to see him, full stop. He had called the evening before his habitual visit. His mother had feared a cancellation since he never telephoned and the weekly rendezvous was as immutable as the succession of days. 'Mum, tomorrow I will bring company ... I will be with my girlfriend ...' This sentence was circled by echoes provoked by interstellar surprise. It was as though thousands of men and thousands of women had suddenly moved into the parents' living room. Bernard's ears whistled: 'Do you realise, he's bringing company ...' Brigitte, in Mireille's imagination, was a sort of countess crowned in one of those countries, strange because they are too hot; she was everything and nothing at the same time. Very quickly anxiety grew in the kitchen. What soup? Routine was derailed; worse, routine had turned into an airplane and was derailing clouds. Mireille was sweating. Above all, the father should not dawdle in the kitchen, he was a bother – and the exasperation rising in crescendo – he had always bothered her, she never should have married him, he was a good for nothing! So Hector's father, far from taking offence, he was a gentle man, sought to reassure her, 'Your soup will be divine, don't worry.' And, in tears, she hoped: 'Really, you think she'll like my soup?'

The following evening ...

Brigitte strung several smiles together. And from these smiles, it was already clear that she would like the soup. Everything else was a piece of cake. False subjects of discussion were covered, at the rhythm of the Stalinist grandfather clock. Everyone had to sit and slurp. It was superb, divine, magical, ecstatic, Brigitte asked for a second helping; holding back many tears, Mireille asked herself who this perfect young lady was. After dinner, that is to say twelve minutes after their arrival, the conversations divided in two: women on one side, men on the other. It was a good old time, tick-tock. Hector embarked on a small discussion on a small subject:

life. His father asked him about his projects in general, and with this girl in particular. He cried, please excuse him, but it really was the first time that he had a discussion of this calibre with his procreator. Brigitte, at her end, was noting down soup recipes, to the extent that Mireille verged on suicide from happiness.

Hector had never seen his parents act this way. More than sentimental consideration, he had perceived the palpitation of the iris; a palpitation wished for throughout his whole childhood. It seemed to him as though he finally had a kind of normal family. Happy parents and happy children. Eating in front of the television on Sundays. And some marriages, idiotically. Ernest already had his wife; he was certainly cheating on her with a brunette from the social litigation department, but this could not be seen in family photos. A beautiful appearance was being constructed. If they were one day to become celebrities, the paparazzi would be seriously bored with this display of happiness. He had a best friend, he had a brother-in-law who appreciated being punched in the face. All that was missing was a date, and the date would be 14 June, a wedding date to perfect this emotional festival. Thank goodness that all happiness wanes, you only have to wait. In the night, Hector and Brigitte were moving towards that direction.

The 14 June was like two peas in a pod with 12 June. Twelfth June always has this proud allure, this ambience of earrings. Ernest and Gérard were nicely getting to know each other; between brothers-in-law you need to help each other. Marcel was also a brother. You do not eat mussels like that and not be part of the family afterwards. He held onto his stomach, suffering from the indigestion of happiness. He was remembering how he had picked this little Hector up from tiny pieces, and there he was now, all handsome, and about to be married. All this was in large part because of him, and no one was coming to congratulate him. We knew it, Marcel.

On her end, Laurence was making numerous new acquaintances, and it appeared as though she knew the location well, as she adored showing unknown places to her acquaintances (places behind the garden trees, behind the shadow of the bride and groom's love). All the guests had grouped in the garden, where, in the sunshine, they would drink to this love's eternal health. It was not possible to prevent the embittered people from toasting. The reception took place before the ceremony, Hector and Brigitte wanted to escape as soon as the yes was pronounced. They had decided to spend their honeymoon in the United States. The mayor finally arrived with his tricolour scarf, in case, inebriated with happiness, their geographic position would be forgotten. Brigitte was white because her dress enrobed her. Hector was concentrating hard. One thing was obsessing him: the rings. It was the last moment where he had to be perfect. He awaited this moment to finally be relieved, the fear of trembling was making him tremble. He was so afraid of not being worthy of his future wife's finger.

A Kind of Conjugal Life

I

Knowing everything there was to know about the United States, the lovers spent a lot of time in hotel rooms. They sympathised with the room service employees. In the airplane, every passenger could see the film he wanted thanks to a personal screen. And upon their return to France, they moved into a large one-bedroom. Thanks to Marcel and Gérard's alternate help, the move was completed in three days. The longest endeavour was the search for the furniture of their dreams. Until the glorious point of their encounter, these two human beings had lived in dust and emotional exclusion. Presently, they wanted to appreciate the modern in order to turn definitively towards the future. Modern impulses often revealed frustrated pasts. Thus were purchased a voice-controlled Hoover, a toaster that does not burn bread, carpets and curtains that change colour, etc. They also bought a goldfish baptised Clockwork Orange (Orange being its surname); and very quickly this fish became a full-fledged member of the family.

Brigitte had obtained her diploma, and was preparing to become a professor of sociology. Of course, she would wear suits; so many students would think of her in the evening, in the obscurity of their revision. Of course, Hector could not stand this thought, jealousy took hold of him at the same time as happiness. By marrying her, he wanted to make her the princess of a kingdom of which he was the only subject. So he suggested something altogether different: create their own company! The idea was brilliant. Hector was turning into one of those 'movers and shakers' with plans for the future. Brigitte also desired to work with him, not to leave him for one second, to love him in a ravenous way. But what could they do? What could they do? she asked him. So Hector was begged to reveal the brilliant idea that had crossed his mind. Standing on the bed, with arms raised, he suddenly cried out:

'For mythomaniacs!'

'What for mythomaniacs?'

'A travel agency for mythomaniacs!'

That was his idea. And very quickly, it was a great success. Hector left Gilbert Associate and Co. to everyone's great displeasure. Ernest trembled with emotion at seeing his little brother fly with his own wings. He thought that one day it would also be his daughter Lucie's turn, and one day further down the line he would die of a cancer gnawing away at his bones. We were condemned to flourish then to rot, and between the two, he spent his life kicking down all the open doors.

They loved inviting the family over for Sunday lunch.

Had Sunday lunch not been created for that purpose? Brigitte was a mediocre cook capable of ruining a ready-made meal. On the other hand, she laid the table pretty well. The same table that the couple sometimes used for love-making. She gutted three turkeys with such clumsiness that he could be proud to have married her. Everyone got on like a house on fire, a postcard. Moustaches were discussed, but Gérard explained to Bernard that you could not climb Mount Ventoux with a moustache, hair holds you back. Brigitte's parents nodded, they were so proud of Gérard when he talked about cycling. When Lucie went to squeeze some spots in the bathroom's filtering lighting, the couple's four parents asked when a baby would be on the way. Ernest thought that children were too often raised as though they were on holiday in Switzerland: 'It's true, they all look like they have asthma! How can we be shocked by the weakness and immaturity of this generation under these conditions?' After this Ernestian theory (that, incidentally, collided against a sort of polite consternation), Hector admitted that having a child was not at the top of their project list. And anyway they could not betray Clockwork Orange, who was beginning to relax in his new aquarium where he could see life through rose-tinted spectacles.

The present project was to expand TAM (the Travel Agency for Mythomaniacs). Within just a few weeks the classes had filled to the brim. If TAM was initially mostly offering the United States and South America, there was now practically no corner of the globe that could not be covered by a course. It was possible, after only six hours of lessons, to make anyone believe that you had spent the last six months in Tajikistan, in Iraq, or for the more reckless, in Toulon. TAM's professors taught, according to their own words, the anecdotes that kill any verbal opposition, that prove our trip without the slightest doubt. And there were even all-purpose arguments: to speak about any country, say that '*nothing is as it used to be*'. People will always agree without really knowing what you are talking about. Well, for the wealthy, the company needed to supply evidence, personalised souvenirs that could even cross the little respected bar of photomontage. Or, for some regions reputed to be dangerous, people could be slightly injured. There was for instance a section: 'Vietnam 1969 with war injury option.'

A newspaper article that discussed a poll taken among a representative sample of a thousand men was framed at the entrance of the agency.

a) *Do you prefer to sleep with the most beautiful woman in the world without anyone knowing about it?*

b) *Do you prefer for everyone to believe you have slept with this woman without it actually being true?*

The result overwhelmingly confirmed that in our society everything is only other people's consideration. Indeed, 82 per cent of the men asked opted for the second answer.

Hector appreciated sitting peacefully on a chair to read an interior decoration magazine. The price of English furniture is insane. He felt good at home, with his wife. Sometimes, boredom took them by surprise. On certain Tuesdays or Saturdays, without surprises, you needed to learn to kill time. It was also in these moments that they understood the stodgy value of sex: the hollowness of existence was filled by boxing themselves in, filling in sensuality. Hector put down his magazine, and, kissing Brigitte's mouth, his happiness sometimes hurt him. It was a happiness from everywhere that surged like a Napoleonic army in Prussia. Thanks to their company's success, Hector and Brigitte moved into a four-bedroom apartment. Every night, the torrid couple made love in a different bed. They really believed that routine was a question of location, not bodies, illusions.

2

It is impossible to know exactly at what moment the thing occurred. It certainly involves the vague echo of a feeling with an uncertain dawn. Besides, Hector cannot be said to have been alarmed in the early days.

That summer was more than a promise. We knew with certainty that the sun's rays would tickle lovers' bodies at a time when everyone was talking about the death of the seasons, a favourite subject of those who *really* have something to tell each other; this summer was not going to betray anyone. Brigitte had put on a very nondescript outfit to do what she called her *cleaning*. Hector wanted to help (their marriage was barely a year old), but Brigitte laughed saying that his help would only make her waste time. (Ah, men.) Hector began humming some words of an old song, Brigitte loved his voice. She felt happy and secure, happy even during the Saturday afternoon cleaning. That summer, they had decided not to leave, to profit from Paris without the Parisians. They would stroll along the Seine, in the evening, with the shooting stars and lovers fixated by their happiness. Brigitte would be a princess. For the moment, she had to clean. The sun's rays betrayed the windows' lack of cleanliness.

The windows' lack of cleanliness: that is the beginning of our drama.

The window is open. The unmistakable sound of women rushing and men rushing to catch up with them can be heard from afar. Hector is sitting reading his interior decoration magazine as usual. He thinks of his living room furniture like he would his children's start of the new school year had he had the time to have kids. Brigitte is busy with her cleaning. Hector raises his head, he leaves the magazine. Brigitte is on a wooden stepladder, her two feet are not positioned on the same step, so that her calves are supporting different weights; in other words, the first calf on the higher step is of a flawless roundness, while the second one is marked by the vein of effort. One is naïve, the other one knows. After the vision of these two calves, Hector raises his head to kiss his wife's hips with his eyes. A slight movement is perceptible, regular waves like the backwash of the night, and all it takes is to raise the head further to understand the reason for this movement. Brigitte is cleaning the windows. We slow down. Brigitte is cleaning the upper part of the windows. It is good work, and the sun is already profiting from the first gaps due to the cleanliness. With finesse, evident in her wrist, Brigitte cleans and hunts down the merest traces of dirt on the windows; nothing should be seen, she aims for transparency. Brigitte reties some strands of hair in her pony-tail. Hector has never seen anything as erotic as this. Certainly, his experience in erotic matters is like the charisma of a fissure. The living room is heating up in the sun. Feeling eyes locked on her, Brigitte turns to check: her Hector of a husband has his eyes glued on her. She cannot see the extent to which his throat is dry. And there, the window is clean. Hector has just been confronted with happiness; it is as simple as that. It should not, above all, be interpreted as macho. Hector is the least macho specimen there is, you know that. It's just that happiness never gives notice. In some stories, it manifests itself at the moment when the knight saves the princess; here, it surges at the moment when the hero looks at the heroine clean the windows.

I am happy, thought Hector.

And this thought was not about to leave him.

After cleaning, Brigitte went with a friend to take advantage of the July sales; she would definitely return with two dresses, a lilac cardigan, and four pairs of knickers. Hector had a rendezvous with nothing, so he stayed seated in front of the clean window. Then, suddenly, he stood up and wondered about the moment of absence he had just had. It had been half an hour since his wife had gone out. He had vegetated, his throat dry, in a dead world. Not one thought had crossed his mind.

In the middle of the following night, Hector thought back to the great moment during which his wife had cleaned the windows. This moment of pure joy, an instant in his wife's life, he thought, an adored instant. He faced the night with a smile frozen on his face. It humiliated all the smiles of his past by its surprising development. All those who experience such an intense joy know fear is not able to relive such a moment. The strangeness of the chosen moment nevertheless troubled him. We sometimes love something in an extravagant manner in the cosiness of the everyday; maybe it was as simple as that. He shouldn't try to understand; too often joys are spoiled by too much analysis. So Hector gently stroked Brigitte's buttocks, her panties were new. She turned around in her tireless femininity, and left her dreams for the man in her bed. Hector slid along Brigitte's body and spread her thighs; she lost fingers in his hair. Stability came quickly; their two bodies were face to face, white and useful. She held on tight to his back, he grabbed on to the nape of her neck. It was impossible to know who was feeling the most pleasure, omniscience ended at the point of the possible orgasms. We only knew that Hector, at the moment of coming, when his head was an empty shell, at the moment of climax, was still haunted by this image, Brigitte cleaning the windows.

The following days went by without incident. Hector thought back to what he had felt, without yet being able to make the link with his past. Believing himself completely cured from compulsive hoarding, he sometimes mocked the crazy way that he had led his life on the periphery of the important. Since he had met Brigitte, any concept of relapse seemed unlikely to him. The evident sensuality, the Brigittian savour, all these new sensations had one point in common: uniqueness. There only existed one Brigitte like his, and in falling in admiration for this unique object, the object of his love, he was abstaining from his obsession. You can collect women, but you cannot collect women you love. His passion for Brigitte was impossible to duplicate.

And the more he loved her, the more she was unique.

Every one of her gestures unique.

Every one of her smiles as unique as a person.

But these proofs did not by any means prevent the possible fascination for any one of gesture. Was that not what was hatching in Hector's mind? A bit too self-assured, he was forgetting his past and the relentlessness with which compulsive hoarding had always returned to impose itself on him. The thought of the window washing bordered on perfidious relapse. Hector had to be very careful, tyranny was watching him, and, faithful to its legendary rudeness, tyranny never knocked before entering.

3

What some of us feared, happened. Clarisse had not been cutting her nails for almost two months when she agreed to do a sexual act, basically quite wild, with Ernest. It cost him several scratches on his back, indisputable traces of a tigress mistress. Big brother of Hector and big dummy above all, Ernest could not undress during almost a good two weeks, and had to make Justine believe that his back was suddenly very cold. The fear of being discovered did not make him regret all the moments when he had kissed Clarisse's shoulders, the tigress hiding in a vast mane of hair. If physical love is a dead end, Justine forced herself into an impasse in the middle of the night to lift her husband's T-shirt, who, it must be said, had slept bare-chested for twelve years. There was something suspicious, and women always spot the suspicious. He had to pack his bags without even finishing his night, and even less this dream that seemed promising (a Chinese woman).

So before dawn, he rang his brother's doorbell to tell him

that he was sleeping with a brunette from the firm, Clarisse, and that his wife, bloody scratches, had just caught him out, 'Can I come sleep at yours?' Well, sleep – he doubted he'd be able to, but sleeping in a hotel, with what just happened to him, did not appeal. Hector found the necessary energy to simultaneously deploy compassion, fraternal tenderness, and the offer of a sofa bed as soft as it was modern. Ernest felt good in this new bed (and if the Chinese woman came back ...) before dignity pulled his mind back to his misfortune.

Ernest had always been sturdy. Adept in the complexities of life, there he was transforming into a Sunday wreck. And it was the worst possible Sunday, the one when they take an hour away. He was catching up on all the years when he had not mourned himself. The poor man was digging himself into a tunnel ... And his daughter! Little Lucie, my God, he would never see her again! He would not even be there when she would come home early in the morning with the red eyes of an inert and depraved teenager. There it was, everything was finished. You should always look at the nails of the woman that you sleep with. What an imbecile! He would only have his work left. He would dive in tomorrow to drown under the files. With regard to his divorce, the saying was already known: cobblers often have the worst shoes. It was the same in this case; lawyers plead their own cases terribly. They often marry among themselves to cancel out this effect. Ernest would ask Berthier to take care of him. He was a fine man this Berthier. Moreover, as a hardened bachelor (Berthier had reached the degree of celibacy where the existence of women is forgotten), he would do everything to speed things up. Between men who were going to be bored stiff in their lives, you needed to help each other. No really, this Berthier would be perfect. He even would have deserved a mention earlier in the story.

Hector was very disturbed by his brother's rough patch, and even more so because of a peculiarity. Ernest, until now the quasi-Olympic champion of happiness, was sinking at the precise moment when Hector was finally seeing life through rose-tinted spectacles. His parents had not wanted two sons at the same time; in other words, they could not both be simultaneously at the same place in their lives. It was almost as though the wheel had turned and that Ernest was going to live, to Hector's great pleasure, a life of depression. Their life as brothers was schizophrenic.

This suggestion of the wheel that turns between the brothers did seem rather absurd, because Hector was not on his best form. Ungrateful periods always lurk behind the joys. This could well seem ridiculous, especially in this context (such a beautiful Brigitte, a company in full expansion, a child on the cards for later), but Hector did in fact seem feverish. He was going around in circles since that morning, and felt incapable of escaping these circles. Brigitte, in a light dress that every summer deserves, had just left the apartment. Hector did not really look like much. He did not even harbour the beard of the tired man; his hairs, hardly masterful, resembled employees on a Monday morning. Even an oyster would have been bored in his company.

A little later, we find him sitting in his armchair again. Atrocious thoughts are circling his mind. Facing the window washed the previous Saturday, or was it a more distant Saturday (the memory occurred so often he'd forgotten when it originally happened and how long it'd been since he'd 'never felt so happy'), he remained silent. Evanescence captured, sensuality caught, he could have died that day. As Thomas Mann wrote: 'He who has contemplated Beauty is already predestined to die.' Brigitte's window washing was a bit like Hector's very own *Death in Venice*. But Hector did not know who Thomas Mann was, so he could survive. Lack of culture saves many lives. Oh, that Saturday afternoon! Mythic moment where time, with respect for such beauty, should have stopped! Hector, facing the window, always and again facing the window, shed tears of joy. Was it possible to love a woman so much? A woman in all the strength of her fragility. It was this moment that he recalled in memory. This moment of washing that he'd not chosen just as love at first sight is not chosen. If all couples return endlessly to the place where they met, Hector was of course allowed to relive the moment where Brigitte had washed the windows. This moment would be the pilgrimage of his love.

So, he spent the day dirtying the window.

Dirtying a clean window, while trying to give the impression that it became dirty naturally, is not an easy feat. And Hector, before reaching the true perfection of natural illusion, had tried several formulas in vain. Through successive trial and error, he had just reached perfection for what must really be considered a new art form. His victorious composition was the following: a few fingerprints cleverly disposed, a fly caught in full flight then squashed right away (speed is of the essence, because an antagonised fly, with its final jolts, creates a more authentic mess than a fly that is already quite dead), a bit of dust from the street and, to crown the lot, an indispensable and light trickle of spit ...

Hector was speaking on the phone with his brother: 'Someone's lent me a studio for the time it takes to get back on my feet. So that's already done.' Hector made a play on words, and Ernest laughed to make believe that he had understood – when Brigitte came home from work. As soon as he hung up he justified his absence from work with a headache. Brigitte gave a hint of a smile:

'You're as much a boss as I am, you don't need to give me any excuses!'

There was no time to lose. Brigitte needed to spot the dirt on the windows. He was immediately faced with one of the greatest challenges of our humanity: trying to make somebody discover something she has no intention of seeing. Hector, in such a rush, thought of saying, in the least conspicuous way possible: 'Oh look, the windows are dirty.' But he rejected this idea, it was not possible. She would definitely have asked him why he, who had stayed home all day, had not given them a wipe ... This could easily deteriorate into a domestic argument and should therefore be avoided. He had to lure her into the living room, and make her discover the pot of roses. After, he was more or less sure that she would clean right away: she would never allow such a window to survive. But it was interminable, the longest day ever. Brigitte had billions of things to do in the kitchen, or in the bedrooms, and when, finally, miracle of the night, he succeeded in luring her to the trap of the living room, she did not once look in the direction of the windows. As though she was doing it on purpose, the bitch. Hector pranced in front of the window, bobbing his head. She laughed at his silliness. 'My husband, the comedian,' she thought. He bitterly regretted not having forced his hand, not having spat out a kind of incredibly visible phlegm. There might still be time, she would only have to turn her back and he would pounce to dirty the window some more! Far too perturbed by the situation, far too exhausted by his yearning, he felt incapable of waiting any longer. He there-fore opted for the most mediocre solution, and grabbed Brigitte by the waist. He suggested they gaze at one of the most romantic views there is from the bay window.

'Darling, if you raise your eyes, you'll be able to see something rather peculiar ...'

'Oh really, what?'

'Well, you know that we can see the building opposite ...'

'Yes, and?'

'And, and, it's crazy ... And look, you can see what is happening in the apartments.'

'Well yeah ... That's what you call having two buildings

face to face. Say, your headache, it's not improving ... *(After a time.)* But this window is absolutely disgusting!'

(Climax: when the hunter captures his prey; the ecstasy of the warrior in his conquest, life is as gentle as sentinels on your skin.) Without surprising anyone, he adopted a small, pitiful tone to wonder:

'Oh really, you think it's dirty? Me, I hadn't really noticed ...'

'I don't know what you need ... I have never seen such a disgusting window!'

Brigitte busied herself with the gentle ease of women who are never caught unawares. Hector, unable to restrain a small erection, walked backwards three metres to slump into his armchair. He looked like an ice cube sliding to the bottom of a gin and tonic, just before floating. Brigitte, not being endowed with eyes in the back her head, did not notice. She did not see her husband, or the trail of saliva that escaped, drool spreading on an otherwise innocent tie.

It was then.

It was then that the telephone rang.

Hector did not allow himself to be disturbed, nothing else existed anymore. Brigitte, after three rings, turned around and asked whether he planned to answer before the death of the caller (so Brigitte was a funny woman). She did not spot the drool – the size of which was impossible to miss – because they were still in blind love.

'Yes, I'll get it,' he quickly said. He could not irritate her; it was as though she were pregnant. The person calling at the worst possible moment deserved at the very least to have his hands ripped off, and his vocal cords, and his hair. Hector was walking backwards, his eyes transfixed by the performance. He lifted the handset, let it agonise in the air for a few seconds, and hung up, humiliating its very purpose.

'It's a mistake!' he shouted mechanically.

He went back to sit down. Suddenly, without really knowing from where it came, emotion submerged him. Sobs swept across his face, just as Magritte's men fall from the sky. Hector did not regret anything. The beauty of that moment had just repeated itself. Without the surprise from the first time, there was, however, more magic this second time, an incredible dose of apprehension, an anxiety of the deception, and, in apotheosis, it was the ravaging of relief and recovered adrenalin. The clean window, the red curtain. Brigitte came down again from the stepladder, but could not move because Hector had thrown himself at her feet and was whispering 'thank yous'. It inevitably concerned a manifestation of her husband's formidable sense of humour, so she too began to smile. She began to smile like a woman who finds the one she loves an idiot.

4

Laurence lifted the dish to get a nose-full of the aroma from the veal paupiettes. She felt good in her comfortable kitchen, and took advantage of this evening among friends to decompress; she would soon be in the finals of a competition critical for her international career. Her coach had given her ten days off, but she had not been able to stop herself hitting the ball, working on her mythic wrist stroke; well, we know. It was Marcel's brilliant idea to invite Hector and Brigitte for dinner. She was happy to see her husband's friend again. She did not really know why, but for almost two years now he had studiously avoided her. Well, she did have some doubts, actually. Hector was scared stiff of her since the testicle fondling incident. However, from her point of view, this had only been an expression of affection. So it was also to straighten things up that she called him to the kitchen.

Socially, he could not refuse.

He entered the kitchen and witnessed the paupiettes' preparation, his face white and blood cold. Or the opposite.

'Can I help you with something?'

'Yes, I would like for us to have a chat, one second ... well, you see ... I don't understand why you've been fleeing me all this time ... When you left for the United States, I thought that it was because of me ...'

In saying what she had just said, Laurence advanced slowly but surely towards Hector, she'd wanted to pacify their relationship, excuse herself for her sexual aggression; however, upon seeing him, this best friend of Marcel's, a low impulse itched at her, an irrepressible impulse like in the time of Racine tragedies. She then rushed towards him, Phedre of paupiettes, and in wanting to catch Hector's testicles once again, her hand collided against a hard surface. In anticipation of that evening, and due to an all-in-all justified apprehension, Hector had protected his crotch with a footballer's shell. Laurence screamed, and immediately, everyone crashed into the kitchen. They rushed to the emergency room, and the diagnosis was unambiguous: Laurence had sprained her little finger. The next morning, this was largely related in sports newspapers: *Laurence Leroy forfeits final*. The two fans she had in Evry cried.

Hector felt guilty. All professional athletes should have the right to fondle the testicles of those they find attractive – with no aggravation. Gérard, before Ouarzazate-Casablanca, must have had a field day. He felt so guilt-ridden, and this burden was too heavy to carry (let's not forget that he already had to bear his abnormal attraction to the Brigittian window washing). The morals of the French would be lowered because of him. With horse riding and fencing, ping-pong is one of our biggest sources of pride. We are a physical people! Yet now we were nothing more than a bunch of sprained little fingers.

What has just been related is not quite exact, and this *hors-piste* of reality must be attributed to Hector. His imagination has travelled towards the worst. Laurence had indeed injured herself, but thanks to her friend the physiotherapist, she had been able to heal, and would take part in the final. Phew!

She was nevertheless mentally weakened, and for the first time in twelve years, she asked Marcel to accompany her. Far too emotional to follow the matches of his darling, he had never wanted to come. In the context of the sprained little finger, he would have to overcome his anxiety. To confront this situation, he had no solution other than beg his friend Hector to go with him. Even though ping-pong was by far the sport that interested him the least in the world, his ongoing guilt pushed him to accept. They would leave this Saturday for the whole day. Hector asked Brigitte if this absence, the first in since six months, at least bothered her. Not at all, she quickly reassured him; she was a woman perfectly able of improvising a whole Saturday, just like that. And then, on the sly, with the most innocuous voice there is, she added: 'I will take the opportunity to do some cleaning.'

The sentence immediately lingered in the air and became the only air in Hector's head. How could he think of anything else? She would do some cleaning, she would do some cleaning. Big flushes of anxiety attacked him. He did not dare ask the question haunting him; he did not dare ask the details of this cleaning. But she stopped any interrogation in its tracks because she added that she would clean the windows. At that moment, and in a totally brutal way, he thought about his suicide attempt. And then, he tried to pull himself together, he was a man after all! The first idea that came to his mind was to clean the windows himself on Saturday morning; at least he would be sure that she would not do it in his absence. Or he could announce to Brigitte that it would rain heavily on Sunday, the announcement would render an enterprise to clean the windows null and void, rain water loved to humiliate clean windows. Dozens of parades were invading his mind, nothing could cause him more anguish than not assisting to a potential wash, it was just not conceivable. He found himself in front of a mirror, and thanks to this vision, he cut short the zigzagging parade of his mind. He was shaking, and in this movement, he was dropping beads of sweat. He felt as though his fate was escaping him again, and that he was becoming a heap of flesh prey to obscure demons. An eternal return was wriggling in him.

We had (sorry) underestimated Hector's propensity to be twisted. It has to be said that the decision he had just taken was somewhat shocking; in any case, for all those who had been unable to reach the initial levels of his neurosis. When he saw himself shaking and sweating a few minutes ago, he had just had a revelation: he should never prevent Brigitte from washing the windows. His problem was not that she was cleaning, but rather that he was not there. Therefore, he considered that he had no other choice than to leave a camera in a nook in the apartment. A secret camera of course, and he would take delight in the images upon his return. There, he had his solution. On Saturday, he could go with a clear mind and support Marcel who was supporting Laurence. Until then, he did not go to work, and bought sufficiently adequate equipment. He did not regret all these moments spent reading magazines about the most up-to-date technology and modern furniture; he was even satisfied that this time was finally paying off. During all these steps, he did not once think back to the old Hector, the one who obsessed on acquiring a specific object. How did he manage not to understand the point to which he had relapsed? His illness, in catching up with him, had blind-folded him.

Thankfully we still had a friend who, again and always, was going to explain our life to us. However, Marcel was not having an easy time of things. Selfishly, he knew that if Laurence had the misfortune of losing the match, the atmosphere at home would be unbearable, and he could always dream of seeing a real shepherd's pie again. It was obviously not Marcel's principal thought, and his whole heart united itself in cosmic waves with the sub-God delegated to the affairs of ping-pong. He was not being haughty: small stomach pains were harassing him. And it is finally because of this discomfort that the two friends ended speaking about the cleaning of windows. Wishing to distract, and thus hoping to diminish the gastric slippages of his friend, trying by all means possible to concentrate on this man who was almost asphyxiating him, Hector thought he was doing well in recounting his latest exploits. So he started to explain how he had hidden a camera on the top of a cabinet, a camera that would be set off at every movement in the axis of a dirty window. His attempt was crowned with a great success as Marcel, shocked by what he had just heard, stopped all his farts short. Aggrieved, he asked for some additional information: how did all of this start, how did such a crazy idea come to him, and so on. The explanations barely over, he uncovered the atrocity of his diagnostic.

'Hector, you have plunged back!'

In a first instance, Hector thought swimming pool. Then, he took his head out of the water to understand the figurative meaning of the words 'plunged back'. He required silence to digest the terrible announcement. Everything tallied, every morsel of his new passion stuck, moment by moment, to his earlier life. This devastating fascination for a moment of his wife, and this irrepressible urge to relive it. He then enunciated this sentence, disconnecting every syllable: 'I collect the moments when my wife washes the windows.' Hector repeated this sentence 112 times. The sweat, the frenzy, he was collecting a moment of his wife. Again and again, the shock of the evidence. And the more he thought about it, the more he wanted a small hit of cleaning of windows; he was already addicted. He tried not to cry, and yet how to not think of this terrible question: was it possible to be another man? In meeting Brigitte, he had believed reaching the wonder of uniqueness, the woman of all unique women in each of her gestures, unique in her unique way of biting her lips, of passing her hands through her hair in the morning, with her grace and elegance, woman of women, unique in opening her thighs. And yet, nothing could be done, always the same mess, gnawing and absurd, always to lead this life of a worm in reduced earth.

Marcel lent him his handkerchief. He promised to take him to Deauville to eat mussels. Everything would get better. This idea of mussels could have finished him off but, in a surprising way, Hector regained some composure. The memory of the wash produced a hint of a smile (a gap in his mouth). The paradoxical malaise of the collector is that he finds the biggest source of rejoicing in his vice. Transformed into a mental collection, the moment of the washing of windows has become his possibility of not living a soft life (during a session of psychoanalysis, he would be told that he is seeking to kill his father). When Brigitte cleaned the windows, it was her refrain, it was the song that lovers sing under the rain. The absurdity of his life had the charm of clichés. Thus, he was not unhappy; all he needed was to think about his secret. To feel good, he had found the solution: not to seek to get better! He was like that, full stop. He liked the window washing of his wife like others like to go to prostitutes while walking the dog. He was going to start a subterranean life for the umpteenth time. Of course, there was a non-negligible part of risk. To film the woman of your life behind her back: we had seen better for the peace of the household.

Marcel loved to buy newspapers when he took the train: simple newspapers where current affairs, summer fashions and celebrities were discussed. Under his elbow, there was a weekly whose cover was on *the strange affair of the disappearances*.[1] Two young women had been abducted in the same Paris neighbourhood. We learned everything about their lives, but there were no elements about the abductor. Hector, still bowled over by his resolution, thought that he would never know the abduction of his personality. They were finally arriving in a city that looked a bit like Saint-Etienne. And Laurence won her match 23 to 21. She was gentle when she won.

---

1   If we mention this affair of the disappearances, it is because it will have its importance in our story. Here, nothing is ever superfluous; we do not support the unnecessary.

5

Brigitte did not notice anything, the camera had been so discreet it was worthy of a wildlife documentary. Hector, upon his return, acted as though nothing was going on, which was incredibly easy since to act as though nothing was going on was the attitude towards which he had the highest disposition. Saturday evening they made love, endeavouring to tire themselves out as much as possible so that Sunday, a day that is sometimes hard to kill, would unfold in the torpor of physical recuperation. Well, they would have done better in abstaining, as a serious (and peculiar for people who consider Sunday as a difficult day to kill) event occurred: it was Mireille, calling in a quavering voice, a soup problem, thought Hector, and in actual fact it was far more serious, since this telephone call announced his father's death.

'Oh my God ...' sighed Hector. And three minutes later, he could hardly feel anything. Except, maybe, some gurgles in his stomach, signs that he was hungry.

Death has its faults, it encumbers the lives of those who are alive and kicking by leaving those who do not die in their arms. A mother, for example. We should always die in groups; it would be like a package holiday. Hector did not really know why all these cynical thoughts were going through his mind, it was perhaps the effect of death, it hardened him in one fell swoop. Hector did not cry, but Brigitte, adorably discerning, understood that something peculiar had just taken place. She approached her man who suddenly had a child's face, and placed a gentle hand on his cheek.

'Is something wrong?'

Hector thought at that moment – was it an echo of his cynical trip? – that he could obtain anything from that woman. When you lose your father, how many window washes can you win?

Ernest was the older brother, so he was charged with taking in their mother. Hector spent the night with them. There was also Justine who had returned to the marital home, after having attempted to lead a single life. They had played out their crisis, and then, lo and behold, everything was forgotten. Hector thought straight away about his story of changing luck. In his mind, Justine's return announced the pending end of his pseudo-happiness. No doubt about it: a karmic threat was hanging over the two brothers: they could not be happy at the same time. (At least the Karamazovs were all three united in the sinister.) Between brothers, you have to help each other. Yeah right, he was not even able to endure a trivial year of misery. He had to re-Justinify himself. To relax, he went out to buy some instant soup and prepared it for his mother. It would lift her spirits, her daily soup. Ultimately, that was far from the case. After the two brothers motivated Mireille to eat a little, at least enough to survive until the funeral, she acquiesced and found herself face to face with a painful revelation: instant soup was good. All these years, she had bought, washed, peeled twelve million vegetables to, at the moment her husband died, realise that our modern society provides delicious ready-made soups. She entered a depression that would only end with her last breath. Hector blamed himself for the blow, and added this new guilt to the sum of guilt-feelings that he had to bear for the rest of his life.

The few days preceding the funeral, Hector had turned around in circles a lot, an attitude that was beginning to characterise him. He was subsiding in his age, and was considering, for the first time, that he did not have children. When he died, who would come to wander around his tomb? Who would come to throw some flowers? No one; without offspring, tombs remain tombs, and never know the cosiness of petals. It seemed to Hector that he had always sought a good reason to have a child, and he had just found it here, in the evidence of his future solitude. He was becoming narrow-minded, obsessed with his vital benefits; we did not really like him in those moments. After reading an article dedicated to the best positions in view of procreating (the hard-working aspect of Hector, a taste for efficient things) he caught Brigitte like an animal in heat. She thought that he needed to reassure himself of his father's death by copulating non-stop. On that point, she was not entirely wrong. But falling pregnant was not part of her plans. So, when she understood her husband's desires for expansion, she admitted not being ready. She suggested a dog, just to get used to it gently.

It was raining that day, it was such a cliché! Death was always a cliché. You do not innovate or show off on the day of your death. Anyway, you are always lying down the same. The women were dressed in black; and the stiletto heels reminded the deceased of the tick-tock of the grandfather clock that he would never hear again. The mother's tears ran slowly. Her past life, and the short life that was left for her to live, could be read on her face. A small plaque was left in front of the tomb:

He had so loved his moustache.

Hector stopped on that word, moustache. His father was in that word, the death of his father was in that word. He suddenly felt the moustache as a weight that was lifting, the hairs were rising towards the sky. He had always lived in anxiety and need, always squashed in the smallness of a living room with a large grandfather clock. The death of his father, he was thinking about that expression: and all his worries were disappearing, all the collections, all the needs to always protect himself; nothing can be expected any longer from a dead father. We become responsible for our shell. He raised his eyes to the sky, always the moustache, and, ahead of the sky, a large window ingrained itself. A large window that Brigitte washed immediately.

6

Like a woman you only undress partially, Hector had waited several days before watching the tape. He had put it away in a calm corner of the living room, and now that he was entering a phase in the afternoon where he was incognito, he could envisage harvesting the third part of his collection. Sitting comfortably, the telephone off the hook, Hector was going to savour this delicious moment. He immediately felt something strange: how to say it, it was the first time that he was looking at Brigitte when she thought she was alone. The change was not vulgar for a non-connoisseur of Brigitte but every deviance in behaviour, as minimal as it was, jumped out at Hector. He found that she stood less upright. It was a question of millimetres, a light futile nothing, but on video all the modifications of the loved woman could be seen. To be honest, watching her was boring. She was not a big hit. At best, she could have been accorded a part in a Sunday night Italian TV film. Hector pulled himself together. Waiting for the ominous moment, he subconsciously criticised everything that was not that moment. Brigitte had to be washing windows, or could not be anything.

Hector pressed on pause, and contemplated every millimetre of the Brigittian calf. He had just had an idea, an improvisation in happiness: he should add music to the images! He thought of Barry White, of Mozart, of course, of the Beatles, of the music of the film *Car Wash*, and finally, he opted for a very famous German song whose lyrics were pretty much like this: '*nanenaay, ich-nanenaay, nanenaay, ich-nanenaay*' (phonetic translation). When you film your wife washing a window, you do not skimp over the details. Everything had to be perfect. Sensual pleasure was a physical science of which everyone possesses his own Einstein. For him, this German music was exciting. Brigitte was wonderful; for the third time, he was watching her in the purity of her feminine deployment. He stopped the tape on several occasions. His eyes, wide open like a mouth before a sneeze, gleaned every particle of the film. Hector was becoming completely dependent on Brigitte's washes, to the point that he was almost feeling a non-pleasure at the satisfaction (difficult sometimes to make love to a woman who is so loved). He was of course still able of grasping the *carpe diem* of a clean window, but like every Judeo-Christian who lives in Paris, he was caught up by a Left Bank guilt-feeling. Satisfied pleasure always had the venomous colour of the collaborationist eras. He felt dirty, his father had just died and he was getting aroused basely. His whole life had been but a masquerade, he was mediocre and shame was walking all over him. Shame was limping all over him.

It was then.

Yes, it was then that the recording stopped since Brigitte stepped off the stepladder and went out of the frame. The next image was Brigitte's return, but this time, she was accompanied by a man. Yes, a man! Hector almost choked, even though no pretzel agonised the horizon of his larynx. There was no time to pause the tape; and it is often thus that the big dramas of our lives begin. The man and the woman (yes, Brigitte had become 'the woman', the sudden impression of knowing her less) talk a few seconds, and their mouths are close, far too close, dirty mouths. Because of '*nanenaay, ich-nanenaay, nanenaay, ich-nanenaay*', it is not possible to hear clearly what they are saying to each other. An almost 'new wave' atmosphere can be discerned in this atmosphere of corporal betrayal. But, assuredly not much of a cinephile, the man transforms into a beast, drops his trousers, and spreads Brigitte's thighs; the act is executed, there is a record in this, in less than twelve seconds.

Stop (Hector stops the tape).

In a first instance, you do not reason, you think of throwing yourself out of the window, you think of the other man's body, you think of the moment when he is writhing over Brigitte. The bastard did not even leave her time to clean the windows; odds are, he's a pervert. And to say that he was with a friend watching a ping-pong match; he had always hated this shitty sport, a sport invented to make men cuckolds. Brigitte's flesh soiled one Saturday afternoon, it reeked of the poverty of suburban trivial events, for all he knows, she had a familial connection with that masculine thing, something consanguineous that would make of this disgusting affair an affair humiliating humanity. He needed to breathe, to take matters in his own hands again, and taking matters in his own hands was to look for this maniac to wring his neck. Only, he did not know anything about violence; he had sometimes fought over objects, but never had the fatal point of physical aggression been crossed. A cold sweat took over him at the memory of the stranger's hairy back, a back as large as a shark's jaw; she was cheating on him with a Saturday neanderthal. The cowardice of his possible reaction to the situation racked his brain. There probably were other solutions. He thought of hiring a hit man, something proper and professional, a bullet in the neck, and then, he would not show off as much with his *ad vitam* limp thing, his hideous thing that had explored Brigitte's mythical interior. But frankly, where could he find a good hit man on a Friday in the middle of the afternoon? He was worried that they would lumber him with an intern who would forget to burn the silent partner's name before pulling the trigger, maybe not even oiled.

Hector had not read Aragon, and ultimately it is not essential to read Aragon to know that sensual pleasure is a dictatorship. The tyranny par excellence that we only over-throw by overthrowing ourselves. So, the idea of finding a hit man, the idea to doing the guy in, are joyously ridicu-lous once the idea of happiness has been brushed against one single and severe moment. To leave Brigitte would irremediably mean they would not see each other anymore; and not to see each other would irremediably mean that he would no longer assist window washing. His intelligence, stimulated by the redoubtable shock he had just experienced, was leading him towards evident real truths. And from this evidence flowed one unique truth: the impossibility of speaking about what happened with Brigitte. The collection 'washing the windows' had to be preserved at all costs; not to put anything in jeopardy, even to pass for a coward. To be a coward, yes. But for pleasure. We could see vice in this, though every sensuality is the vice of another: sado-masochists must find missionary position of amateurs truly vicious. Hector was trapped by his sexual pleasure. He therefore did not have a choice, and Brigitte would come home that evening, he would look at her right in her eyes, and he would give her his biggest smile, the one tested on their wedding day.

We liked it, that smile.

A Kind of Decadence

I

It is no more stupid to stay with a woman who is cheating on you just to see her wash the windows, than to go around the globe just to see for one instant the beauty of the earlobe of this beloved woman, than to commit suicide like Romeo and Juliet (this Juliet must surely have been a champion of window washing), than to go pick edelweiss for his Belle du Seigneur, than to go to Geneva just for a day to look for the Ritz that does not exist, than to need to live in sensual bubbles, than to love you with that way of looking like a Stalinist moustache, all that is the same, so Hector had no reason to feel guilty for his small sensual drift. Everyone has the misfortune of loving. Moreover, making a woman believe that you do not know she is cheating on you facilitates peace in the household. After the afternoon he had spent, Hector was not against a pit-stop in falsehood. He could not look at her quite like before; to be honest, it was even far worse than that, since he had a constant vision of the lover. When he looked at his wife, he saw a woman whom a boor with the face of a Czech apparatchik had fitted into. As there was a good film on TV that night, it was ok. They would be on the couch, couches are pleasant, they are like newly-adopted children, and they would share a beautiful moment of gentle Americanisation. Brigitte found Hector's attitude strange. She tried to know what was wrong with him, and inevitably, in the great tradition of sudden panics, he chained several 'nothing, nothings' that rang, it must be said, quite hollow. Desperate, he quickly glanced towards the window, and considered its deceiving cleanliness; he would still have many days, maybe even weeks, to wait beneath the sweat of another man. He lied, saying that he had a headache (it was the third time he was using the same excuse that evening) and, once again, Brigitte dissolved two aspirins in a glass of water. It was his sixth that evening, and as luck would have it, he started to feel the beginning of a headache.

Friday nights systematically flow into Saturday mornings (no capacity here to surprise us). And one week ago, the preceding Saturday, Brigitte had been cheating on Hector in the atrocious conditions that we know. As though by chance, that morning, hardly awake, she asked about her husband's schedule for the day (her adultery was being tuned like a Swiss watch). Did he honestly have the look of someone who has a schedule? Hector never had anything planned, and especially not the days when his wife was seeking to gain information in view of copulating while he had his back turned towards his schedule.

'I don't have anything planned ... and you?'

You needed to have balls, to be able to answer like this. But madam did not waver, nothing, not a drop of sweat (although he, in such a situation, would already have been raising his left arm to keep coronary thrombosis at bay). Women are fascinating. In truth and lies, women are fascinating. So Brigitte had to do some grocery shopping, and then, in late afternoon, from five until seven, she would see her brother. Gérard was an easy scapegoat, what could she possibly be doing with him on a Saturday afternoon? No, it was not possible, nobody saw their brother on that day. Brothers are mostly seen on Tuesday lunchtime. So Hector's heart skipped many beats (by the by, he was already beating a saying). He was entering head-on the jolt of dignity that every cuckold knows well. He wanted to do nothing, and wait nicely for the next window washing; but when he listened to his wife deploy her timetable of lies under his nose, he then wanted to flush her out. Men are as small as their resolutions: he had not lasted half a day. Brigitte had hardly left their so lovely apartment (they had been happy once) than Hector picked up the phone to call the alibi brother. The associate confirmed, of course. How had he believed one moment that he would drop her? Families always hide adulterers in caves, they are the Jews of love. Apparently, her alibi was plausible, they had to buy a gift for their parents' wedding anniversary. The bastards, they were also in on it. The whole family must have really been laughing behind his back, his ears were burning like hell fire. He should have been wary, what an idiot! Thank goodness that he had been hit with the passion for his wife washing the windows;

without this opportunity, he would never have known anything about the family plot that was being woven around him. He would presently have to be very careful, and, why not, place more cameras.

Hector had just called Gérard, and he had been obliged to find a pretext for this telephone call. Gérard was not the kind of man you call just like that, something concrete was required. Roughly, and in a state of panic, Hector did not find anything other than suggesting a bike ride in the late afternoon. By sweet-talking him, he might have cracked. As we know, he confirmed his sister's alibi with surprising aplomb, in spite of the cycling temptation. On the other hand, he had not thought through the collateral damage of such an attack. Gérard, with incredible good humour, suggested they go on this bike ride right away; it's true, why postpone until tomorrow what we can do now? This Gérard was a real moron (now that the marriage was going down the pan, Hector was no longer going to rhapsodise on his brother-in-law's bikes, and on this race of North African minions that the first doped-up European cyclist could have won), but as he was a moron whose muscular mass was inversely proportioned to his neuronal mass, he should not be provoked, as they say. Hector had to put on some shorts, and they gave him the appearance of a right-wing candidate in municipal elections. He looked in the mirror and found himself thinner, it was not necessary to come closer to spot the protuberance of some of his bones.

Gérard kissed him on the cheek, they are family. 'I have just done a hundred press-ups with my left arm', he added by way of welcome. They immediately went to the cellar to take the spare bike that Hector would use, a bike that would reveal itself slightly under-pumped to ensure that the friend didn't transform himself into a potential rival. In the staircase, they crossed a smiling neighbour; and if usually Gérard was always incredibly friendly, this meeting occurred in disconcerting coldness (an express handshake). You could enjoy cycling with your brother-in-law but to snub a neighbour was not on. Something was amiss. Hector had enough time to perceive incomprehension in the neighbour's eyes, but let that sensation escape instantly. It was a bit later, when the Bois de Vincennes looked like a merry-go-round because he was turning around it so much, that he was caught up by a double notion:

1) This neighbour was incontestably a friend of Gérard's that he pretended not to know.

2) If the second notion was even more diffuse, it was on the path to becoming clearer. Hector had the feeling that he had already seen that man; however he had never been to his brother-in-law's before this business of alibi verification. Was he a celebrity? No, you do not snub celebrities in staircases. His azure eyes, these eyes, he knew him, he knew him from having seen him many times ... Ouarzazate-Casablanca! It was one of the cyclists from the podium!

They rode some more, Hector glanced at his watch: that was now almost twelve minutes they were pedalling. Why did time seem so slow while they were cycling? It is the perfect sport for all those who think that life passes too quickly. The calves and thighs in action were airing the mind, it was a wonder that Gérard had remained such an idiot. It was then that, in a very intelligent way (our hero), Hector faked discomfort and stopped on the roadside. As a great professional of sport medicine, Gérard strung a few invigorating slaps together to restore the dying man to health.

'If you want to continue, go ahead, I'm going to stop,' agonised Hector.

He blamed this discomfort on his lack of training. After all, he had not committed a sportive act since 1981, on the march to celebrate François Mitterand's victory like everyone else; François Mitterand was since dead as the result of a long illness hidden for a long time from the French, and he had never had a concrete occasion to perform any sport again. Cycling was suddenly beating ping-pong on his list of despised sports. Gérard seemed at a real loss because, for him, the idea of the family is as sacred as a king; he was not allowed to abandon a family member on the roadside, it was proscribed in the rules of his religion. But as his main God was cycling, he went back for a few solitary circuits. Hector went to sit down on a bench to recuperate, and it was on the bench that the Machiavellian thought came to him: to denounce Gérard. It was every man for himself, and if Brigitte's whole family was uniting against him, he needed to use the weapons at his disposal, including the basest of them all, denouncement. He was defending his interests like the first animal arriving in times of war. He was not really going to be scratched dirtily and die a slow death without ever seeing the window washing again.

After an effort of three quarters of an hour, Gérard returned, hardly out of breath. He had climbed, and especially gone back down like never before; the regulars of the bistro at the Porte de Vincennes, Chez Kowalski, could even testify of this capacity to go down. It required a minimum of intelligence to lie, and Gérard's intelligence, so sought-after by all his human attitudes, was only leaving crumbs all over the place. He therefore had not thought of buying some chewing-gum. Hector recoiled his nasal horizon by a few centimetres to be able to follow his brother-in-law's exploits. He stopped him short:

'I know you did not win Ouarzazate-Casablanca.'

'...'

'And if you don't tell me who is meeting your sister tonight at five, I will reveal everything to your family ... And to all your alcoholic friends!'

'...'

If Gérard was a tad mythomaniac, everyone accorded in finding him nice. He was not used to being attacked (there had already been a polemic on this race, but the affair had been settled for a long time, and in his mind, buried; of course, lies are Lazaruses always ready to raise themselves in the miracle of a new light ...), and that was why his capacity to answer jammed up for a moment. There is a saying that speaks of the calm before a storm – hmm – as soon as he had recovered from what he had just heard, he broke out violently against Hector. He broke two of Hector's teeth and then stopped:

'The best thing is to sort this out at my place!'

Hector sought by all means possible to retract what he said, but he had gotten on Gérard's sensitive nerve. Ouarzazate-Casablanca was his whole life; the pedestal on which he had let his days run. No negotiation was possible; in two beats and three movements, the two samples from this same family found themselves in Gérard's cellar. A bit earlier in the day, when they had come to find the spare cycle in this very cellar, Hector had not noticed the enormous poster for the film *The Silence of the Lambs*. Suddenly, in the flash of a second, a vague reminiscence of a pseudo-cinephile discussion came back to him, where Gérard had practically had tears in his eyes in evoking the sequestration scenes of his favourite film.

2

In this space close to agony, Hector thought back to those moments where flesh had finally delivered him from the identical infinity of his life. The unforgettable details of the first moments of his love for Brigitte were misty in the vapour of a sovereign feeling, subtly tyrannical. Although he could almost no longer feel the blows that Gérard was striking him (there exists a strange stage where pain joins sensuality), the blood in his mouth was transforming itself into cleaning product for windows. He was not begging, he was not saying anything. Bound like a bootleg ham, he was awaiting death quietly on a riverbank, with the hope that there would not be any delays like last time. Of course, he would not die; if Gérard had little experience in excessive violence, he knew, and this thanks to his movie knowledge, that all that was required was to scare the infamous traitor who was threatening to speak. He was intending to stop his punches as soon as he would hear the eternal promise of his victim's eternal silence. But in lieu and place of this silence, was face to a smile. Hector, plunged in an ecstasy judged perverse by his torturer, was discovering a quasi-masochistic pleasure. Gérard did not understand: in *The Silence of the Lambs*, the victim was not smiling; well, ok, she was being dismembered, but with what he had thrown at him (his fists were hurting him), this brother-in-law smiling with all his teeth minus two seemed like a hallucinating vision. Gérard suddenly began to shake in front of the one he was torturing. And, a minute later, threw himself at his feet:

'Yes, it's true ... I never won Ouarzazate-Casablanca! Sorry, sorry!'

Hector returned from his sensual voyage. The pain from the blows suddenly imposed itself everywhere. He promised not to say anything to anyone; in any case, he was not even certain to still possess a tongue capable of forming words. He tried to get up, and Gérard helped him. A great incomprehension about what they had just lived through made them feel uncomfortable. The struggle had opposed two nice men, both of whose sensitivity had been attacked: the potential glory for one, the potential erotic for the other. Two nice men trapped by the ambition to safeguard their lives from sorrow at all costs.

On that common point, they embraced.

Hector went home walking, vaguely finding geographic landmarks in his drift. People were staring at him in the street, which had not happened since the day of his suicide; he could therefore definitely classify that day with the anti-prize list of his glories. He walked into a pharmacy to buy something to disinfect himself with and stick some bandages on his face. The numerous wounds forced him to cover himself almost completely. On his way out, he heard a voice compare him to the invisible man. It was stupid, he could not look like the invisible man, because no one had ever seen the invisible man.

At the bottom of his building, Hector lit a cigarette to the great astonishment of his lungs. He smoked like an adult, swallowing plumes of stillborn smoke. After the cigarette, if no woman was falling from the sky, he could try to continue to live normally. His ideas were taking back a coherent form in their sequence. He was regretting having wanted to blackmail the cyclist. Everything would be simpler if the women we love did not wash the windows. Overflowing with love, he would have resigned himself to this sexual misconduct and would have forgiven her. They could maybe have gone to see a psychologist for unstable couples? They would have been told why they need other bodies so much to advance, why they are carnivores gorging themselves with alien flesh. They would have sat on a couch and the doctor would have also wanted to see them separately. To compare, to close in on the problem; to understand why Hector's wife, such an erotic woman in her homeliness, felt the urge to be taken standing in the familial living room. There was surely a reason for this.

Hector regained consciousness of his pain. He could not believe that he had thus returned to the glorious times of his pitiful episodes. How had he accepted such humiliation? The window washing was sublime, but did he have the right to lower himself to this point? Just as in the greatest moment of compulsive hoarding, he was squashing his dignity for an object. That was his problem, he did not value himself more than an object. He was nothing, and at the moment where he thought this thought he walked in front of a mirror to really remind himself of his invisibility. I am an object, he thought. To get cured, he would maybe have to try to collect himself! He wanted to smile but his smile was confined in disinfectant bandages. He did not want to go home; he looked to see if the lights were on. No, no one. His wife was maybe having an orgasm at that moment.

Hector had no more tears.

Far from his wife's hypothetical orgasm, Hector slipped on a soft and odorous mass. There were many dogs in this almost completely Chinese neighbourhood. Four adorable onlookers stopped in front of the non-artistic skating amateur, not to help him up, but to regret in concert to have missed such a fall. He stood up, more frightened than hurt, as they say; but often, we forget that *la peur*, the infamous fright bone, is very small and located near the hip. At the doctor's the following Tuesday late afternoon – 'Doctor Seymour will try to see you between two appointments' Dolores the temporary assistant said – the radiologist he insisted on seeing, confirmed a fractured *la peur*.

It had now been a week that he was officially a cuckold. He had the right to count what he wanted. He even had the right to celebrate this title of glory. Many men would dream of being cuckolds, just so that they would also be able to cheat without guilt. Evidently, he was adapting his sudden theories to his state of future hermit. There was no doubt such an end would come for they said that women were far more whole than men. She would leave him then. He would be nothing more than a dumped man. The idea of the empty bed that was etching in his head was making him choke. His love was going to go and leave the sheets cold. Coffee would also be eternally cold. (How on earth could he make the coffee?) He would spend his days in front of the television, and his pyjamas would sport indelible stains. He would forget that he too had been a man capable of shaving in the morning. And no, it's not possible! He was refusing this destiny of timorous depressive; he needed to consider his life with more ambition. He was going to change, he had to change! Because of love he felt ready to forgo the window washing. He would forgive the hairy body of that other man, the happy body of this other absurd brain. He would forgive the erring of the flesh, the need to entwine together non-stop to exist! Everyone knew the meaning of these deviances. So they should be accepted without seeking to understand.

Take her by surprise, he could not see any other strategy to conquer his wife again. To open her eyes with astonishment. He thought of greeting her with a sumptuous dinner, she who would be returning full of unknown sweat. Adultery could also be cured with love. She had liked Laurence's roast that other time. Unfortunately his resolution ended with his intention, for he was not in any state to be able to prepare anything by that evening. He would therefore take her to the restaurant, and to celebrate this incredibly surprising outing, she would wear a princess's dress. The restaurant would be happiness. There would be candelabras that would plunge the evident cracks in their relationship into semi-obscurity. This idea of the evening where everything would start again lifted the spirits that we had thought dead in Hector. He entered his building, forgetting his physical appearance. The odour of dog shit persisted so much that we had the right to wonder what it could possibly have eaten.

Luckily, he did not cross anyone in the stairs.

Unluckily, entering his home with his head in the clouds, he surprised all those who were seeking to surprise him for a good hour at least and who, with this superb art of vigilance, had started to shout: 'Happy birthday!' He recognised Marcel, Brigitte, Ernest and the others. You had to be a real arsehole to be born on that day.

Hector was exactly the kind of man who cannot stand people organising birthdays for him; in his head, all he could see were conspiracies. They had talked behind his back; they had arranged the surprise like others hatch treacherous plans. Without counting that he had not helped them with his surprising initiative: to go cycling with Gérard, what an idea! The bastards had panicked a little; but they had landed on their feet like pros. He didn't even know how old he was. All these incredibly good-humoured people would have inevitably baked a cake that would remind him. That's why they were all there, to celebrate the backwards count, to pack down his false youth in the Chantilly. The atmosphere darkened due to his appearance. People wondered what had happened to him. Hector realised that his appearance had reached a rough patch on the one day when he was finding himself among all the people he knew. This was the incontestable sign of a disastrous social life. Nonetheless, the collective fall in spirits was ephemeral. When you organise a surprise birthday party, you are forced to overplay the good humour (you need to be a guest to be able to sulk). They all felt responsible for inflicting such a humiliation on Hector. So they succumbed to cheesy smiles. Not allowing themselves to be discouraged, the family and friends belted out the classic song. Here, there is never any surprise, people always sing 'Happy birthday to you ...'

As always (it's a bad habit), Hector wanted to die on the spot. The shame that all were inflicting on him was immeasurable. He who had decided to change, he who had decided to accept the nascent nymphomania of his lady-love, he was being unjustly crushed in his attempt to become a responsible man. They were all playing him, from the beginning. To start with, his parents put him on this earth just to avenge themselves of his brother's departure. You do not produce two children with twenty years difference, you are not allowed ... He was not moving, transfixed in the malaise of being him. At that moment, he would have given anything to have protective objects all around him, immense collections of stamps or cocktail sticks that would hide him from the eyes of others. In the middle of them was his wife, his Brigitte. So she was not with her lover; she still loved him a little. It was a vague sensation, a tiny nuance. Nevertheless he felt the gentle echo of hope: she still loved him ... She preferred his birthday to corporal activity with another. Finally, it was not so useless to be born on a specific day, and to celebrate that day. She loved him ... He wanted to live his future like a castaway on a desert island on that little piece of love that was left.

Mireille, his mother, approached him to find out what was wrong with her darling. There really needed to be a lot of people for her to call him darling. This brutal return to reality had no consequence other than to make him escape. He clambered down the stairs, but not all of them. In other words, he missed a step, and spilled onto a neighbour's landing after a rather spectacular forward roll. In the impossibility of getting up, he felt like a wild boar injured by a drunk hunter. Brigitte, who had run after him, squeezed him in her arms to reassure him. Hector was shaking. He had not broken anything but that the roll added to the few disappointments of the day had scared him. This day that was beginning to seem very long to him. 'Don't worry my love, I'm here...' Reading her husband's pain with precision, she added: 'Yes, I will tell them to leave.'

So the guests left the aborted party.

Back in their apartment, she laid him on the bed. It hurt him to find her so beautiful, and his other pains grumbled at this useless surplus. She undressed him and passed a lukewarm sponge over the bruises on his body. Not knowing where to begin, she did not dare ask what had happened to him. She could not understand why he was trying to smile at her either. He was so happy that she was taking care of him. She must love him if she is being so gentle. She even kissed him on a wound in the strange hope that her acidic saliva would have the effect of immediate healing. Her lips were also sucking the venom of incomprehension, was it really necessary to try to find out? In any case, Hector could not speak. Brigitte, on the other hand, had to speak.

'Does your state have something to do with the video? ... Well, it's not that ... I am having trouble understanding why you have not said anything to me ... I've waited all week for you to talk to me about it ... It was fake! Special effects! You only see the man from the back, and we are pretending. The day you left, I spotted the cameras ... And I did not know what to do. I had wanted to call you for you to explain yourself. I asked myself whether you were insane. And then, I preferred to get revenge by directing some adultery ... And you, you did not say anything! For a week, you did not say anything ... You believed I was cheating on you, and you stayed quiet ... I can no longer believe that you love me ...'

So Brigitte had not committed a sexual act in their living room; it was a put-on. She had endured a week of self-restraint. Hector's smile stretched until it almost split. The slowness of his mind prevented him from comprehending that it was now his turn to explain himself. To explain why he had filmed the woman of his life.

'Why did you film me?'

She added this question, and irrepressible tears drowned it out. They were swimming in incomprehension. Hector sought to reassure her with his eyes, to tell her how much he loved her. He would have wanted to make her eternal through his love. And it is in the heart of these unrealised spheres that he was thinking about his answer. Did he have the choice? Could he do anything other than tell her the whole truth? If she loved him, she would know how to understand him, right? Do you leave a man who admits loving more than anything the way that you wash the windows? It is a declaration like any other, a particular devastation of sensuality. Women like original men, right? Well, to know what women like, you need to know at least two, thought Hector. He rose, and took Brigitte's hand, this hand he had seen before seeing her face, you often meet the woman of your life in front of books. Both of them were walking towards the living room. And the man pointed to the window with his finger, and the woman, facing the window, remained in confused. Up until the moment he explained: 'I wanted to film you cleaning the windows.'

A Kind of Sensuality

I

Persuaded that no one would ever want to see him again, Hector was readying himself to experience the solitary fate of summer rain. We are not allowed not to pick the surprises that others plan for us. Brigitte reassured him like only she knew how. She had called family and friends to explain to them the reasons for the sudden escape. She had invented a fall in the street (a concrete alibi). They had to understand, right? Who would not have done the same? Only Gérard had appeared dubious, of course, but as he often did not comprehend what people were telling him, his sister did not notice this dubiousness. For the moment, they needed to save face, to make others believe that there was nothing serious, that falls were frequent in our slippery society. She was even forcing herself to laugh. Women always manage to stay on course during the chronic drifting of men. Now that she had staved off the others' interrogations, she was finding herself confronted by her own. Immense, major interrogation, interrogation without the merest echo in the history of interrogations. How to react to a man who secretly films you, who films you washing the windows? After the initial anger, she could not consider him anything other than sick. And you do not leave the sick, especially not those you love obsessively. For she loved him, there was no doubt about that. They shut themselves away in their apartment for many days. She had been a nurse. He would have liked for this illness to last longer, just to eternalise the sensation of being held in the palm of his beloved's hand. The illness was making an object of him. He felt occupied like a vanquished country, no longer in the least responsible for his body. The couple soldiered on in the silence of these days; this phase was surely necessary before they explained themselves and thought about the future. The silence was bandaging the evidence of their love. Without words, their gestures were of an accentuated tenderness. Their hands spoke in the manner of Chinese shadows, miming gentle declarations. In these moments they were brushing euphoria. A kind of ecstasy of primitive beasts. The last days, Hector was wincing to show pains here and there. He allowed himself to drift on the crazy dream in the absence of words, of people and of things. A life in the contemplation of his wife.

They were not going to be hermits eternally. Brigitte wanted and needed to know why. Why he had filmed her, and especially why he had not said anything. Two 'whys' whose responses would determine their future. Hector was very bad at explanations. Speaking about himself caused him anguish. He was afraid she would not understand him and that she would take a plane to leave the country, and then trains and ships moving unfathomable distances away from him. The first word that formed in his mouth was the word 'relapse'. Slowly, he managed to evoke his past in compulsive hoarding, the defeat with Nixon, the lie about the trip to the United States ... In short, he was stammering his life like a novel. And finally he admitted he wanted to collect the moments when she was washing the windows. It was his new collection, the most absurd, the craziest, the collection that was ruining his stable life, but however, in evoking it, his heart was palpitating. He had never been as happy in a collection as in this collection where his wife was the heroine. Lucid about the drama that was playing out, he did not reject the sensual power of such a moment any less. Brigitte hesitated a moment to be flattered, before admitting the absurdity of such a thought. Her husband was sick. Well, all the same, few women were able to drive their husbands crazy just by washing the windows ... And the more she found that what she was listening to was tantalizing, the more she knew that she would not leave him.

Hector was sobbing. His life had only been a long illness. Guilty of having relapsed in such an atrocious fashion, it was up to him to face up to his responsibilities (this expression made him nauseous) and to leave. He did not have the right to spoil their love. Up until this terrible collection, he had never implicated anyone in his illness. He needed Brigitte; without her, the collection did not exist. The equation was of a rare perversion. Dramatically, he searched for his suitcase. 'I have to leave!' he shouted, raising his fist. He looked like an actor auditioning for a role as an understudy. Those who leave in such an ostentatious manner never leave. His wife began to laugh at his shticks and at the weirdness of their relationship. She had dreamed, in the hours of youth where clichés reign, of a life with a strong and protective man; together, they would have had children: a football-loving son, and a daughter who plays the piano badly. She had never dreamed of a husband who would drool in front of her way of washing windows. However, she liked this idea more than anything: every second of her life really did not resemble any already chewed-up idea.

'Drop your suitcase!'

Hector obeyed from the word 'drop'. She put a finger on her husband's mouth, a well-known sign that incites silence. She took him by the hand, and suggested they walk towards the living room. They slowly passed their corridor. And in the room where the shock of the washing had occurred, she asked in a *Lolita* voice: 'So, you like it when I wash the windows?'

He bobbed his head.

She continued: 'You know, my love ... All couples have their fantasies and madness ... And to be honest, I still prefer this to you taking me to an orgies club ... Plus it's quite practical since it also allows me to clean the windows ... No, I do not see anything that bothers me, I even think that we are a relatively normal couple ... And me, your wife who you love, it's my duty to satiate your fantasy ...'

On that note, she climbed the small stepladder magnificently anticipated for that effect. Hector, who did not agree with the word 'fantasy' (he was dealing with irrepressible and pathological impulses, fantasies could be lived without), did not really have the possibility of producing any sounds since, as soon as the movement of washing started, his throat became dry. There was a sublime particularity in that opus propelling itself in the heights of his collection: this particularity was the actual announcement of the moment. His wife had looked him straight in the eyes to tell him: 'I am going to wash the windows for you ...' Without a doubt, this washing belonged with the masterpieces; not to say the masterpiece of his collection. Yes, it was apotheosis. And he understood the major ingredient that, on top of the announcement, was killing him with pleasure: the lack of guilt. For the first time, he was delighting in his sensual fascination in broad daylight. He was no longer buried in the obscurity of his peculiarities.

Once the last fleck of dirt was cleaned, Brigitte stepped back down towards her husband. Hector did not know how to thank her. Brigitte interrupted him:

'Don't thank me ... Once again, it's normal for a couple ... And if we want our marriage to function, you too will need to satiate my fantasies ...'

Hector's mind stopped one moment on that last sentence. He had never thought that his wife would have any fantasies. Brigitte was far too pure for that ... Or else, her fantasy was perhaps to turn on the light, once, like that, while they were making love. To turn on the light, just to be a little crazy. That had to be her fantasy. Brigitte, so gentle, Brigitte with such divine calves, Brigitte who was approaching his ear to reveal her fantasy to him: Hector managed to fall even though he was seated.

Hector appreciated this newly discovered quality in his wife: situational intelligence. She was placing both of them on an equal footing. She was transforming herself into a sexual master of ceremonies to save their relationship. In equalising the relationship, she was polishing their difference, making their borders porous. Brigitte had infinite resources of compassion; so suddenly compassion was becoming vital to make cars roll – the United States would no doubt attack her immediately. She was kissing Hector in the darkness, their embraces were becoming less and less sexual; they loved each other in their solitude. They remained entangled the longest time possible. At his request, she would wash the windows.

Their life would be like that.

It was too soon to see their friends and family again (they had feigned another trip to the United States to avoid explaining their social imprisonment). They decided to repaint the whole apartment white and let, more or less voluntarily, the paint overflow. They became white for a few days. White lovers on a white background.

Their love was modern art.

Of course, everything was not so rosy. To live as a couple with a washing of windows from time to time as their only occupation was monotonous. Having a child could have fulfilled them, but it would take too long to come, they wanted something to do right now. To be honest, they were in a phase of reconstruction, and nothing could be predicted in these moments of healing. All the other collections of his life had ended one day or another, but this last one seemed to assume a mythic ease. He could not get over seeing Brigitte wash the windows. It was always the same movement, and yet so different every time. The motion of the wrist, the small sigh between the lips, according to the day and the season, you did not wash the windows in the same way. His collection was enriching itself visually, not like any other. Rain spiced up the lot on occasion; a storm made the washing such a delicate art form. But once the excitement passed, he fell back to the whole breadth of malaise. He would only have to wait for the next time, the next urge. Hector was regaining the state he had known all his life, this perpetual anguish of the collector, drugged on the hits of dictatorial power.

Brigitte had to leave to go shopping, they needed to eat. In the aisles of the supermarket, she was an ageless woman. A boy was hitting on her at the fruit and vegetable counter, she was a desirable woman, many hands would have fantasised of penetrating her *décolletage*, to take her breast and forget their fingers there. This supermarket flirter offered to take her out for a drink, to jump her in a scummy motel. She was imagining herself legs akimbo, surely she would have taken some pleasure, like that, by chance. Some hit the spot with chance. And then after, nothing, they would not discuss literature; and when he would draw the curtains, he would not flinch in front of the inevitably dirty windows of every motel. It was already boring her. She wanted to wash windows.

Hector was also going out. He loved to take the sixth Metro line. There were many sublime moments on that line. He found the compartment's windows to be dirty. Imagining his wife cleaning those windows, he was remembering how awkward it was to have an erection in public places. There was something for which to be happy in that (a certain idea of a return to life). Nevertheless, in the tunnels, he felt some hot flushes. He had the impression that he himself was becoming this Metro that was being swallowed by black holes. Hector got off at the next station. Chance had it that this station was called 'Montparnasse-Bienvenue'. Without this little word of '*bienvenue*', he would surely have put an end to his days. It was a nominally human station, one of the rare underground places where, in the face of emptiness, we did not have the physical fear of being pushed in the back.

4

Slowly, their lives were alive again. They tried to laugh at the turn of events in their story. They would have a small washing, then they would go to bed. Hector was regaining an appearance worthy of a semi-modern man. They had officially announced their return from their holiday, everything was going to start again in beautiful clarity. They would finally be able to satiate Brigitte's bizarre fantasy. They had not been able to do so previously since this fantasy required being invited to their friends'. They had chosen Marcel and Laurence (but did they really have any other friends)?

Marcel opened his arms as wide as possible, as far as the walls allowed him. Laurence, all sparkling, greeted the couple hurriedly because she was still very busy in the kitchen (a roast). Hector, already uncomfortable, was dreading the evening. But his wife had already offered him so many washes that he did not really have a choice. Brigitte suddenly seemed perverse, the smile of an easy woman could even be detected on her face. It was as though she had always led this type of ceremony, and, sufficiently sure of herself, she took the time to relax her partner. For that, she had no alternative than to do what followed: while both couples were sipping a Marcellian punch, a zest of lemon and three zests of surprise, she was going into raptures about it being such a beautiful apartment. Laurence, even if she was a high level athlete, was never insensitive to compliments regarding her way of keeping house. She felt proud that a woman respected her. But very quickly that feeling was wrecked by another of Brigitte's observations: 'On the other hand, if I may ... I think that your windows are not quite clean.'

Hector spat out his punch. Marcel started to laugh until the moment when he crossed Laurence's glare. After almost having climaxed from the compliments on her interior, she took a slap in the face about her windows. She stammered that she had not had enough time ... Well, yes, she had neglected them ... In short, she was asking for forgiveness. Brigitte told her that it was not serious in the least, and apologised for her frankness, but frankness was a pillar of friendship, wasn't it? Brigitte, pushed by her audacity, rose towards the window.

'If you don't mind, I am just going to pass a quick spritz for this living room to be perfect –'

'But you're crazy!' Laurence was up in arms. 'It's up to me to do it! We are in my home!'

In an impulse that he could not suppress, Hector shouted: 'No, let Brigitte wash the windows!' Then, understanding the peculiarity of his remark, and also the sudden way in which he had become inflamed, he continued, less proudly:

'Yes ... Erm ... She likes that ... washing windows ... Well, it's just that she doesn't mind ... Well, you see ...'

What Laurence and Marcel saw was that they had invited maniacs for dinner.

Brigitte had managed to pull a fast one. Hector was suddenly excited, and ready to satiate his wife's fantasy. But when she turned, she was confronted by three still faces. Marcel and Laurence were gazing at her intensely. It was strange that her attitude, doubtlessly daring, provoked such an effect on her hosts. Fine, it was not really the done thing to criticise the cleanliness of a place where you are invited; even less to want to remedy the situation. But there it was, it was almost a game, there was no reason to freeze. No one was talking, so she felt obliged to justify herself: 'No, but it was just a joke!' Suddenly, Marcel and Laurence cheered up, and came back to reality without really knowing what had just happened to them. They laughed, understanding Brigitte's sense of humour. They sat at the table.

Hector was not very hungry anymore. His wife had excited him too much, and then nothing. He had to have dinner, even though he was still fixed on this uncompleted washing, or at least too expeditious. Thankfully, socially speaking, the subject at dinner was focused on the United States; a subject they unfurled mechanically, like in the good old days of mythomania. And then the roast was almost ready, so, true to the ritual, Laurence called Hector to the kitchen. He rose with a sigh, resigned for his testicles to be groped. As usual. More and more excited, this time he took the initiative, and placed his hand on Laurence's breast. Shocked, outraged, she slapped him on the spot: 'What the hell is wrong with you! Fat swine! ...' He was speechless and brought out the roast. Still shaken on his way back to the table, he could not believe what he had just discovered: nymphomania is a one-way street.

Brigitte had washed the windows, Hector, too turned-on, had received a surprising slap; this dinner seemed very promising. And the fantasy was not yet put in motion. The fantasy was dozing very near the dessert. Before that, he had to digest the roast that was a smidgeon too dry. But with what had been said with the aperitifs, it was out of the question to criticise anything. Everything was exquisite, but could we, for the twelfth time tonight, have a bit more water? 'Do you find it dry?' worried Laurence. 'Of course not,' the dry throats answered in unison. This roast could have been drowned in an ocean of sauce before being eaten. Finally, the dessert course ended this pitiful dinner with a floating island in the form of mediocre apotheosis. The island was actually struggling not to sink and Marcel, as an amateur of one-liners, rebaptised the thing a floating Titanic.

Brigitte hesitated; she was no longer certain of wanting to satiate her fantasy. She could especially not guarantee that this sensual urge was not a response to the washing. A vital means, according to her, of equalising their relationship. To be honest, in remembering all these erotic moments in the darkness of her room of virgin adolescent, these moments where she touched herself in a still imprecise way, she did sometimes have strange images in mind. She imagined a man who she would love, a man who by love for her would be able to ... No, it was not possible that such a thing could have crossed her mind ... Everyone had their fantasy, she repeated to herself while drinking a bit more of the thankfully treacherous punch. Her vertigo progressing, she took courage, and her crescendo desire, for once, would not agonise in frustration ...

She gave Hector a sign.

Then.

Then he rose abruptly and began to undress.

In prevision of what was predicted, he had worn a simple shirt and trousers without a belt. Thus, he was naked in a few seconds. Terribly awkward, he glanced over at Marcel amicably. The latter who had gathered the secrets about the washing was not really surprised. On the other hand, Laurence overplayed the prude (oh really) by covering her eyes. Hector's genitals were quite short genitals, only a tad cumbersome. Brigitte was more and more excited by the idea that her man was the target of these looks. (Laurence did remove her hands to analyse the Hectorian anatomy.)

'Can I ask what's happening to you?' asked Marcel.

'Nothing ... It's just that I wanted to have your opinion about my genitals. I could only allow myself to ask such a question to friends. It is very awkward for me, but I would like you to be honest ...'

'Listen, you're taking us by surprise ...'

'Oh, I thought so ... you find it small?'

'No, it's not that,' Marcel reassured him. 'It's just that we do not have many points with which to compare it to. For my part I haven't seen many other than mine ... And I don't think Laurence saw more than two before me ...'

Laurence almost choked. Then became angry: 'OK, this behaviour is just unsuitable! You come to eat dinner at our house, we're not in a swingers' club! But if you want to know, your genitals are average, no more, no less ... It is without interest, it has no particular quality ... It seems a bit flaccid on the pre-testicular zone ... *(getting carried away suddenly)* The gland for its part is slightly dichotomous ... You have everything of a premature ejaculator ... Well, I can't be entirely sure ... *(shouting)* In any case, you're a sprinter! There is no doubt about that! It's a sprinter's dick!'

She stopped abruptly when she looked at her table companions' bewildered faces. But, very quickly, the strangeness of that moment was engulfed by the strangeness of the whole evening. There was no more energy to focus on the details (well ...).

Hector was on the lookout for a sign from his wife; she allowed him to get dressed. On that note, they got up and left, warmly thanking their hosts for this delicious evening. To be honest, they were not going to linger after their act of terrorism. Moreover, as is usually the case, once genitals have been unveiled, there is not much left to say. Marcel and Laurence blamed their friends' sudden extravagance on their recent trip to the United States. Americans have ten years advance on us, Marcel affirmed. I would not be surprised if soon all men were to show their things at the end of a meal.

The following summer, they would surely go to Chicago.

Thus Brigitte's fantasy had been that Hector show his genitals. More precisely, her fantasy was that her husband's dick be a topic of conversation, that everyone analyse it like an insect under a microscope. She had loved his little face all embarrassed like a darling little man. He had been so brave that she would wash the windows all night if he wanted. They had both satiated their fantasies. They were finally a couple like any other (were they going to consider buying a house in the suburbs?) They decided to walk home. They were walking hand in hand in the moonlight, crossing all these other couples in love who were walking hand in hand. Paris is a fantastic city for those who love each other with such a commonplace love. Midnight. The Eiffel Tower sparkled with precision, there were always civil servants behind the magic. And it is on the bank of the Seine that Hector had the following intuition: 'Was it really your fantasy?'

Brigitte laughed.

'Of course not, that wasn't a fantasy! My fantasies are a lot simpler than that ... My fantasies are to make love in a cinema or in a lift ... I just wanted to know what you were capable of doing that for me, to prove your love ... After all, I am going to be washing windows my whole life to excite you ... little pervert! So I wanted to make sure that you deserved it ... Come, I have a feeling the windows in our home are dirty ...'

5

Everything was like in the time of their best days. Hector wanted to take Brigitte to the library, to breathe in the foetus of their love. Their hands would naturally find each other in front of the *Atlas of the United States*. Hands did not have a brain, but a memory of love. They separated at the entrance to be able to create an element of randomness in front of the book. Brigitte thought back to this book by Cortázar where the lovers walk in the street until the moment where they meet – finally. She had read it the day of her eighteenth birthday, while she was on holiday at a slightly fat uncle's house. Passing in front of all these students, she skimmed the memory of her youth. Her life seemed surreal to her, and yet in contemplating all these static napes, she understood the point to which she loved her life that was so out of the ordinary. The surreal was a language that tickled her heart. She started to walk faster; it was the moment in films where they zoom in on the heroine. Nothing existed other than the movement of her legs. Music always ruins these scenes.

Applying music to women should be forbidden, their silence is their melody.

They rediscovered themselves in front of the book, and kissed in front of the red spines.

Often it only takes slight happiness to no longer notice the misfortune of others. In the present case, it was actually the opposite. Ever since he had understood his brother's pain, Ernest had grown closer to him. The day of his birthday, he had not believed the alibi of the fall (he had been a witness to his little brother's drifting so many times). Hector had told him everything. In persuading him that they were a couple like any other, Brigitte had removed any guilt-feeling from him. He was now able to evoke his fascination for the window washing. Weird fantasy, thought Ernest. Hector then specified that he was again and always dealing with compulsive hoarding. His wife was regularly satisfying his desire to allow him to survive.

'You are the happiest of men!' raved Ernest.

Hector seemed surprised, and asked whether Justine did not satisfy him sexually. For the first time, they were having a conversation about their rapport with women. Ernest, in wanting to talk about himself, began to stammer. The appearance of his successful life transformed itself into an uncertain, almost blurry, mass. He had never allowed himself to be a topic of conversation. To be honest, he had never found a human being able to play the role of best friend. So his newly beaming brother pushed him to confess.

Justine was not the problem. Justine had a body that

would have made any teenager fantasise, as well as any man who took himself for an eternal teenager. She had an unusual style in bed. But time, in its most clichéd tragedy, had thwarted their erotic games. Ernest was lying to himself; he knew it had less to do with the passing of time than his unalterable love for women. He had cheated on her with Clarisse, and the marks of her nails had almost put an end to their marriage. Perhaps things ought to have happened this way? By weakness (marriage makes you weak), by fear of a certain solitude common to these situations, they had found each other again. She had forgiven him, which meant that she had not been able to envisage a life without him. She remained persuaded that this woman had been his only mistress. She was wrong; Ernest had not ceased creating all sorts of stories to live out. Obsessed by women, their movement and their grace, he could not recall any moment of his life where a woman, unknown or almost known, had not haunted him. During his lunch breaks he sometimes walked in the street just to see women walking. This tyranny in fresh air made him a slave seated in the sensual dictatorship.

Why was he telling him all that? Hector found this story very common. He did not think there was anything pathological to such a passion. Many men loved women in an excessive, hysterical way. He did not understand that Ernest envied him for his fixed passion. His passion for the washing was monogamous. Not only did he only love his wife, but in addition he loved a precise action of hers! For all men exhausted by the incessant movement of stiletto heels,

Hector seemed like a restful oasis. What he considered a pathologic tyranny was a sterilised paradise. Ernest longed to love Justine insanely when she washed the windows. He too wanted to experience sedentary sensual fascination.

Alone, Hector felt disgusted. The people we admire do not have the right to expose us to their weaknesses. This brother who had been a role model had just flown away like a deflated balloon. His wife had stopped him feeling guilty, his brother had just mythified him, he who had been the fifth wheel of a social coach had suddenly become a stable man. At that pace, it would not be long before he would be considered charismatic. '*A stable man*': the expression fascinated him. People would soon ask him for advice, and he would know how to answer. He would read the pink pages of *Le Figaro*, and would finally vote for the Right. While he was daydreaming (you would think that they had spread the word), Gérard showed up unannounced.

'My sister's not here?'

'No, Brigitte is not here.'

'That's good. It's you I came to see.'

Before, no one ever came to see him unannounced.

Hector and his brother-in-law had not seen each other since the famous blackmail affair that ended in torture. It goes without saying that no one else knew about this; enemies in violence often unite in silence. They both maintained a wonderful memory of their sportive, and extra-sportive, afternoon. They hugged an instant too long for this Saturday. Gérard scrutinised Hector's face, and, as a connoisseur,

admired his scarring prowess. There was practically no sou-
venir left from the beating. Not even the teeth; two new
ones filled the void with the charisma of their calcium.

Hector offered a coffee, or any kind of beverage that
would prove his convivial spirit. Gérard, for many weeks, had
thought a lot. His brain, not being in the habit of such a use,
almost overheated. The motive of his reflections: the lie of
his life. It was not possible to continue like this! He was not
allowed to be loved and admired for false pretences. Before
his brother-in-law's threat, he had however forgotten that
it was a pure product of his mythomania. He had rehashed
his false exploits so many times that he had persuaded
himself he had won Ouarzazate-Casablanca. If everyone
believed him, it had to be true. And then, there were the
friends from the photomontage (the neighbours): they too
used the photo to prove their presence on the podium of
the famous race. So the three of them recalled the race from
time to time, inventing more and more extravagant details
every time. How not to believe it in such conditions? Until
the day Hector had come to shake up the myth of his life.
After the attack, he could no longer look at himself in the
mirror; you did not cheat on the other side. He remained
persuaded that his life, without this event, was not worth
anything in others' eyes.

In others' eyes.

Hector repeated this expression in his head. Everything
seemed very simple to him. His whole life, in accumulating
the most absurd objects, he too had wished to appear
important by building a material identity for himself. Raised

by a moustache and a soup, his benchmarks had produced hot air. Ouarzazate-Casablanca was a collection like any other. Every person found his fantastical nourishment. The guiltless Hector explained to Gérard the extent to which he should not say anything. He needed to assume and conserve the sources of his happiness.

'Are you happy when you talk about this race?'

Gérard's lit-up face was worth all the talk. He was not allowed, under the absurd pretext of transparency, to remove himself from his greatest climax. For this was his way, the admiration he provoked in the eyes of those he loved. The search for enlightenment could seem sane, but it did not necessarily make you happy. We should not seek to annihilate our lies and impulses. To admit them should be sufficient. He thought back to his brother and his suffering under the dictatorship of women. He could now find the words. Gérard was observing Hector's face. After a silence, he confirmed that he should above all not admit anything. It was advice from the one who had wanted to denounce him! He understood nothing. And it was a feeling that Gérard knew well, not to understand.

Convinced by his brother-in-law not to say anything, Gérard breathed easy again, judging absurd these introspective weeks. He knew deep down that he would never have been able to confess. Like in the Romand affair, he would have been forced to gun down his parents while telling them the truth. His sister finally came home. He found her beautiful, but did not comprehend her full radiance at that moment. It's true that she was feeling better and better. Brigitte threw herself on her brother, so happy was she to see him. She felt his muscles, and surmised that his recent disappearance resulted from a great occupation to tone and tighten his athletic physique. He answered that she was entirely right, not without having winked discreetly in Hector's direction. The latter gave him a knowing glance. When you live on a well-oiled lie, things roll really easily. Others spend their time making hypotheses, asking questions, so that all that the liar needs to do is to answer yes or no.

Brigitte, as a sublime homemaker, was never taken by surprise when a familial guest invited himself. There were always two or three nibbles (stylish expression) that could be heated hastily. She could even be heard laughing in the kitchen, alone and happy. 'Is she not slightly bordering hysteria?' her husband asked himself. And then, he thought of something else, not to drift towards another urge for washing which would have been awkward in front of Gérard.

The phone rang.

'I'm in the kitchen, can you get it, my love?'

Hector stood up. It was Marcel. He was not angry about the nudist dinner. What a relief! Hector had not dared call him after what had happened; he was far too embarrassed. Marcel's voice was incredibly sparkly. Laurence was very close since her heavy breathing could be heard. She whispered: 'So, what's he saying?' Marcel had placed his hand on top of the receiver to answer Laurence: 'Just wait, how do you want me to talk to him, if you stick to me like that! Let me first relax the atmosphere!' If Marcel had always been incredibly nice with Hector, this conversation seemed to surpass all these moments of niceness. We could frankly say that Marcel was sucking up to his friend. He was saying that it had been an age since they had seen each other, he missed him, the four of them should go on holiday together, and soon another dinner (not one allusion to the exhibitionist scene), etc. Finally, he asked how Brigitte was.

Marcel stopped and caught his breath. Yes, how is she? Hector admitted that he had detected the beginnings of hysteria in his wife, and laughed. Marcel quickly joined in the laugh. Finally he dared to ask: 'Well, Laurence and I, we would really like ... well, this could seem weird to you ... that Brigitte come back to wash our windows ...' Hector burst out in laughter; it was incredible having such funny friends. And in seeing Brigitte go out of the kitchen, he hung up because they had to eat.

Once seated at the table, Brigitte asked what they had wanted, and especially if they were angry for the other night.

'Not only are they not angry ... But Marcel just made a joke, asking if you want to come and wash their windows!'

'Ah that's funny. They are taking their revenge ...'

Gérard did not understand anything about this conversation, so he took matters into his own hands, and evoked Ouarzazate-Casablanca, against all odds.

6

Brigitte visited her parents. She tried to see them once a week. When Hector did not use it as an opportunity to go to his mother's, he joined Brigitte with pleasure. His parents-in-law would have been ideal parents. Simple, kind, attentive, it was even possible to discuss this, that and the other with them. Since a few months ago, they had aged terribly. Especially the father who couldn't easily walk anymore. His whole life he had adored leaving the conjugal home to go on walks, more or less long. He often went to smoke cigarettes in cafes, and play cards while telling misogynist jokes. His relationship had surely held together because of these escapades. Not being able to walk anymore, what bothered him the most was incontestably to see his wife all day long. Old age reduces couples' vital space. You ended up on top of each other, as though you were preparing for a concession. At that age where there was nothing left to say to each other, it was necessary to string platitudes together. Brigitte took the role of referee during these visits.

She relished the good points, and did not seek to reconcile them. Her father spoke less and less; it hurt her not to be able to find any topics of conversation that interested him anymore. He never wanted to talk about the past. And finally, neither about the present nor the future. So, she would observe him, this old man who was her father. His face creased by skin as tight as the time left in his life. Far from depressing her, watching him made her think more than ever that she had to profit from life. Her father's face, in its decrepitude, had surely weighed in her attitude during her marital crisis.

Brigitte always turned up in a really vivacious way; and, before sinking back to his daily nothingness, her father would sigh: 'Ah, that's my girl!' She would go out shopping for groceries with her mother, she always brought gifts to enliven the place. During her last visit, Brigitte's mother had alluded to their wish to leave France, to go to a home in Toulon. It would clearly be a great deal more difficult for her and her brother to go to see them; was that not a distancing strategy, like plopping down in front of death's door? She did not really want to think about it, she was focusing on concrete things. She spoke again about Mrs Lopez, the adorable cleaning lady her mother had fired for an obscure reason: 'She does not know how to do anything as it should be!' It was maybe a way of punishing herself for not being able to do it anymore. Brigitte lost her temper and said that they really needed to find someone else. They weren't really going to embed themselves in filth? She asked her father what he thought: he did not give a shit. So Brigitte did not have any other choice than to give the place a quick hoover, and dust the furniture. When she saw the filthiness of the windows, she did not dare. She smiled, especially in remembering the dinner at Marcel and Laurence's. And then, she launched into it. The context was so different!

In seeing his daughter get busy, her father got angry at her mother: 'Next week, I don't want to hear anything about it, you are going to call Mrs Lopez!' That was exactly what Brigitte wanted, to put some life back into this place, get her father to invest himself once again in their daily lives. She washed the windows so well that her mother was surprised ... She said to herself 'You would think she does this every day' without knowing how right she was. Her husband kindly asked her for something to drink; it had been almost three decades that he had kindly asked his nagging wife for anything. His throat had suddenly become dry. She was thirsty as well. However, she was sure she had drunk a glass of water not five minutes ago.

After two minutes of tremendously efficient washing, Brigitte turned around. The vision reminded her of Marcel and Laurence. Her parents, for the first time since so long, were sitting next to each other. United in contemplation.

'How beautiful you are, my daughter!' exclaimed her mother.

The father, for his part, felt embarrassed, encumbered by a sensation as gentle as it was unhealthy. He could not allow himself to admit it – it was his beloved daughter – but it seemed to him that he had felt a slight twinge of excitement.

She had such a gentle way of cleaning the windows, so ... how to say it ... well ... so ...

'Maybe we don't have to call Mrs Lopez ... if you don't mind my darling ... you could clean the windows from time to time ...'

Brigitte had perceived emotional fragility in her father's tone. His feverishness was touching, Brigitte agreed to do it. She had punctuated her agreement with a delicious pout, in the manner of naughty girls who are always forgiven. After having washed the windows, she kissed her parents with tenderness. She felt that something strange had happened. You could believe at that moment that they were finally going to be happy. Her father made an effort that had seemed inhuman to him until now, in pulling himself off his armchair to sit down straight at his wife's side; on the porch, they made signs together to say goodbye. On the way home, Brigitte let sweet thoughts drift inside her. It seemed to her – and it was a sublime lunacy – that she suddenly possessed the gift to keep them alive.

7

There was an hugely erotic *je ne sais quoi* in her. Brigitte washed windows like no other. After having seen her parents in such a happy flush, she admitted the oddness of what had just happened. After her husband, the addict, and her friends who wanted to make her return, it was the third time that she provoked pleasure close to orgasm by washing the windows. Her father had had the same look as Hector. She had felt discomfort that was diminished immediately: she unconsciously knew that she alone was responsible for the transient fascination provoked. Every human being had to possess a fabulous erotic potential, but rare were those who were able to find it. After her frustrating adolescence, and her first years as a woman where she had thought herself unable to appeal to a man, she had become a sensual power. Excitement was slowly rising. Everything was making sense. People stared at her in the street, she was hopping, and seconds later, she was still. People probably thought she was insane.

Hector did not want to have a siesta today. He tried, in vain, to find something original to do. Thankfully, Brigitte walked in, shouting: 'I am incredibly erotic! It's my fault!' As the man of the house, Hector assumed his responsibilities. He stroked his wife's hair. He had to reassure her straight away; had he not detected in her the beginnings of hysteria? It's true that was not very clear; everything was getting muddled in her brain, she was trying to explain to her husband that he had not relapsed. Since they first met, and as he had hoped, he was no longer affected by compulsive hoarding. He tried to make her sit down, and to serve her a glass of aged bourbon, but there was nothing he could do, she was shaking him, repeating: 'But don't you understand?' He shook his head, worried. She finally understood everything (women) while he needed a bit more time to understand (men).

So Hector had never relapsed. In meeting Brigitte (the woman's body was unique), he had been cured from compulsive hoarding. But, poetically, he had fallen for the only woman who possessed an incredible erotic potential when she washed windows. In wanting to relive this moment at all costs, in going as far as filming the important moment, he had thought himself irremediably affected, though he had never been a man as much like every other.

It was not possible to love passionately and desire to accumulate more objects. Hector had always been persuaded of this. He was a reassured man who had just learned of the end of his illness on the day when he was trying to avoid a siesta. From today, Brigitte would never again wash the windows; he had to be weaned off them. The couple studied possible methods, and six months later Brigitte was not washing the windows to satisfy her husband's desires anymore (they used an American method that spaced out the washes – Americans had the art of considering obvious techniques). Brigitte occasionally, without telling Hector, washed the windows for her own pleasure, like that, as a kind of masturbation. On those days, when he came home, he felt that the windows were clean; his old reflexes. He tried not to think about it, it was not always easy. The bonded couple were faced with other beginnings of relapses from time to time, and they thwarted them with grace.

Everything was now in the past.

Brigitte and Hector formed a stable union that had resisted terrible events. They were beautiful (in any case, they found each other attractive), they were relatively wealthy, they no longer had any real psychological problems (two or three phobias persisted here and there but they certainly would not deserve a book), and they had redecorated their apartment a short time previously. So the project vaguely alluded to on numerous occasions and always pushed back resurfaced at the right moment: the project of making a baby. The expression seemed heavy, terrifying. People called it the fruit of love. To have a child, they first needed to make love. Brigitte calculated the correct dates, explaining to Hector that it was always better to procreate on a Thursday. It was a day that he was fond of. He rested himself properly on Wednesday, and rendered a great performance on said day.

Hector had never been as proud as the day when he found out he had aimed right. The announcement was celebrated fittingly, and Brigitte was going to grow larger progressively. She wanted to eat strawberries, and was nauseous. Hector did not like strawberries, they made him nauseous. The future parents were thinking about their child's future, about his brilliant studies, and the soft drugs he would perhaps be allowed to smoke. From the seventh month, Brigitte became really very fat. She was asked whether she was harbouring a football team (people are often very funny). The couple stayed at home all the time. Hector went grocery shopping, and in the supermarket aisles, he did not even think about collections anymore. His child. He only thought about his child. They had decided not to find out the gender. Hector had an irrational fear of everything that concerned biology; he had not accompanied his wife during the sonograms.

And it was highly unlikely that he would be present at the birth.

But when the day arrived, she begged him to stay by her side in the labour room. Drenched in sweat, and with anarchic cardiac palpitations, he bravely overcame his anxiety. His wife could be proud of him; then, he thought it was more up to him to be proud of her ... Brigitte let out screams, her legs akimbo. So that was it: the miracle of life. The midwife announced that the cervix was half dilated, which meant that there was still one half left to defeat.

So the cervix was opening millimetre by millimetre; every human being, on arriving on Earth, acted like a star. We were an occasion, a happy occasion. The child was profiting from its final moments of great fulfilment, and he was right because there were few chances that he would one day experience the same sensations again; unless he were to bathe naked in freezing water after having drunk three litres of Irish whiskey. Hector stepped outside. Everyone was there: his mother, Brigitte's parents, Gérard, Ernest and his family, Marcel and Laurence ... Maternity drew in all the protagonists. They were supporting Hector, reminding him that fathers are the adventurers of modern times. He liked that turn of phrase; he asked himself who the idiot was who had come up with such bullshit, but it was agreeable to him. And it is true that he looked like an adventurer with his three-week beard (he could not shave anymore because, in solidarity with Brigitte, he too had prepared a suitcase to take to the hospital on the day of the birth; he had put his toiletry bag in that suitcase). He thanked everyone for coming, and promised to return as soon as there was some news. What a man he was, you could count on him in the great occasions. He was going to become a father, and he felt that it was a role that fitted him.

Brigitte screamed, so the epidural was intensified. Hector was by her side once again, he appeared serene. He thought that his wife was beautiful like a woman who is about to give birth. She was pushing harder and harder. The midwife cut a strand of hair from the child whose sticky head. Hector contemplated this strand with such a powerful emotion ...

In an ultra-fleeting way, he could not prevent himself from thinking about Marcel's collection. It was a reflex from his previous life that he did not entirely master; even if he no longer collected anything, he continued to think about collections very often. Well, it was within the space of a second, then he thought: if it's a girl, here's a strand that would be the jewel of Marcel's collection ... And he concentrated once again on his child's progression; this extremely intelligent baby had aligned himself perfectly to get out. The second midwife was applying pressure on Brigitte's stomach to help the child get out. The head finally appeared, almost in its entirety; it looked like a cone. Hector could not see anything of his child yet, and already it seemed like grace incarnate to him.

Accompanied by cries from the push, the child came out and also cried. It was placed on his mother's stomach ... it was a girl! Hector shed the most beautiful tears of his life. He went out one second to shout in the corridors: 'It's a girl!'

He gazed at the marvel emitting little cries in her mother's arms. My daughter, my daughter, Hector could not think about anything else. He had just reproduced himself. His daughter was alive; alive and unique. He had read in specialised books that children stay on their mothers a few minutes before they are taken for their first bath. Strangely, the scene had not lasted longer than thirty seconds. The second midwife had taken his daughter without even asking him to come. Many books explain that if the father is present, he gives the baby its first bath. And here, nothing. No one had even looked at him ... He had hardly had the time to observe his daughter. He was still holding Brigitte's hand, and she suddenly squeezed it very hard, screaming. It was as though they had gone in reverse.

In the waiting room, all the family were embracing each other. A girl, it was a girl, they were repeating in chorus. Hector was not wrong: they were going in reverse. His mind foggy, he could not yet mentally put his finger on what appeared like a strange concept to him. Brigitte who was bordering exhaustion was supported by a new nurse, she needed courage. She squashed Hector's hand. He was finally able to discern the evidence: twins! She had not said anything to him, but she was not pregnant with one but with two babies! This time, he almost fainted. The midwife advised him to sit down. His emotional state was bothering everyone. He thus observed the birth of his second child. This time, it was a boy! Hector kissed his wife, and like for the first daughter, the baby was placed on his mother's stomach.

'But you had not told me anything ...,' spluttered Hector.

'No, it was a surprise, my love.'

Hector threw himself in the corridor and shouted: 'It's a boy!'

This new announcement plunged everyone in confusion, and especially Gérard who was examining this insane equation from every angle: 'But it's a girl, or is it a boy ... It can't be a girl and a boy ... Well, yes sometimes, it can happen ... But not so young ... Or else ...' He asked a nurse passing by for an aspirin.

Drunk with happiness, the father on a cloud and the mother in a daze, the parents had just settled in another world. Hector wanted to follow his son in the room where he was being bathed, but, once again, a midwife took the child. In a small voice, Brigitte confessed to Hector: 'I did not tell you everything ...'

'What?'

'We're having tripleeets!' A contraction hacked the word.

Brigitte went back to push with the little strength she had left. She was an exceptional woman, three children in one go. Hector looked at her as though she were an extraterrestrial. He loved her in a superior love. Courageous, she brought a second girl to the world and, relieved, burst into tears. The little girl went to join her big brother and big sister for the medical exams, and a few minutes later, the midwife announced that the three babies were doing wonderfully. She added that she had rarely seen a delivery of triplets occur so easily.

The three children were placed side by side; they seemed identical like three pieces from a collection. Hector could not believe he was the progenitor of these three human beings. He kissed his wife, and in that kiss he bestowed all the courage they would need. *Fathers are the adventurers of modern times*, he thought back to this expression. With three children in one stroke, he at least deserved the designation of hero.

End

November 2002 – August 2003
Ouarzazate–Casablanca

The author thanks the Centre National du Livre for its help.

David Foenkinos is a recipient of the Hachette Foundation's Young Writers' Grant 2003.